# The Postman is Late
## (A Neighborhood Watch Mystery)

Vicki Vass

This book is fiction. All characters, events and organizations portrayed in this novel are the product of the author's imagination or are used fictitiously. Any resemblance to actual persons—living or dead—is entirely coincidental.

For information, email the author at vvass@yahoo.com or visit her website at vickivass.com.

Tedeschi Publishing

Cover design by Elizabeth Berry MacKenney
Berrygraphics.com

ISBN: 978-0692552353

# DEDICATION

To the real Grandma Jan who keeps watch over our neighborhood. We
sleep sound at night knowing you're always on the watch.

## Chapter One – Jan's Notebook, Today

Some neighbors might say I'm set in my ways but what other ways could I be set in? After 75 years on this planet, I'm not about to change. I have a routine, and I like to keep to it. My mornings start the same way every day. I have my first cup of Jewel Eight O'Clock Extra Bold coffee and then head outside. Today is no different.

I checked my watch and glanced up and down South Linden Avenue for Michael's dark blue Dodge Neon. Seventeen houses on the east side, eighteen on the west. Ranches, split levels, bungalows, one or two colonials sprinkled in. Woodland View, Illinois, is fifteen miles west of Chicago. The thirteen thousand, nine hundred and seventy-two residents of Woodland View sleep sound at night, hidden from the danger of the big city. And, my street, Linden Avenue, is a dead-end street surrounded by the DuPage County Forest Preserve. We are an island to ourselves.

I looked up and down the street again for the Neon and checked my watch, a little after 6 a.m. and the newspapers were late. This wouldn't do. I tapped my foot against the curb. Patience isn't my virtue.

I walked to the corner to see if I could spot Michael. It's not like him to be late. At the corner house, Mr. Hiro was out early raking leaves in his wildflower garden. I waved to him. His English is worse than my Japanese so we have an understanding and communicate through smiles and nods. Some of the neighbors complain about his native wildflower front yard but I appreciate his hard work and tenacity. And, if he misses any weeds I make sure to yank them out when he isn't looking. I can't help it if sometimes I can't tell the weeds from the flowers.

6:07 a.m. still no newspapers. This would throw my whole day off. Each weekday is precisely organized according to my schedule. Tonight is Bunco night at the VFW hall. Yes, I had a full day. The Dodge Neon squealed around the corner off of Spring Oaks onto South Linden. Michael slammed on his brakes when he saw me standing in the street. "So sorry, Grandma Jan." He handed me my *Chicago Tribune*.

"Michael, no need to speed. We'll make up the time," I said, taking the newspaper and sprinting alongside his car.

Michael is a nice young man working the extra job delivering newspapers to care for his new baby. As he threw the papers on my neighbors' driveways, I strolled behind and delivered them to the doorsteps. Years ago when I started delivering papers, some of my neighbors thought I was stealing them. I explained that I was bringing them up to their doorstep to save them the trouble of walking down to the curb. Now they greeted me with a smile. I needed the exercise and it isn't as if it was every house like in the past. Most people these days get their news on their computers or their phones. I still like the feel of paper though I don't like the smudged ink on my hands.

I headed back to my house, a no-nonsense suburban split-level. Like most of the houses on Linden Avenue, it was built during the 1960s housing boom. It was time for my eight-year-old great-grandson Daniel to leave for school. His mother, Meg, my granddaughter lives in the main house with my daughter, Valerie, and her husband, Bill. Valerie built a second floor addition for me. I have my own little apartment complete with back stairs so I won't disturb the rest of the family. It is quite cozy with its six by six foot porch. From my perch, I can see into all the neighbors' yards. The nice family next door has a beautiful garden. Those are the Andersons, Jeffrey and Debbie, and their 20-year-old son, Tony. On the other side is Anne Hillstrom and her white Persian cat, Sassy. I'm not what you'd call an animal lover but Sassy and I have an understanding. I appreciate cats because they keep to themselves and aren't as messy as dogs.

I made my second pot of Jewel Eight O'Clock Extra Bold coffee. I finished the rest of the pound of bacon I made earlier. Valerie constantly warns me about cholesterol. It isn't anything that I worry about. I weigh the same 90 pounds I have since I was a showgirl at the Sabre Room. That's where I met my husband, Gino, and Frank Sinatra. But that's a story for another day.

I relaxed until 11 a.m. Now it was time for Gary, the postman. I went back outside. Next to Anne's house is Bob Wilson's house. He is on oxygen and can't leave the house to get his mail. So I deliver it to him every day, rain, snow or shine. I was more reliable than the post office especially during the week when Gary was on duty. The neighbors constantly complain to me about how Gary tries to shove packages into their street side mailbox instead of delivering them to the door.

I went and checked my mailbox. There was nothing in it. Not too unusual for Gary. He was late. I breathed in the spring lilacs that Anne planted along her driveway. Sassy popped up in the picture window. We nodded at each other in recognition.

12:22 p.m. I checked the mailbox once again. Still empty. Watching for the white and blue Jeep, I walked back down to the corner. The neighborhood was quiet. Most people were at work. My daughter, Valerie, was at her real estate agency. She wouldn't be home for hours. I walked north down South Linden Avenue as far as I could before entering North Linden Avenue. I was trying to avoid the other Jan, North Linden Avenue Jan. She'd have something to say about something. I didn't have time for her nonsense.

I stopped in front of the bungalow that was foreclosed upon months ago. It is next to Mr. Hiro's house. The nice young family with the large standard poodle just disappeared one day. Now the lawn had gone to seed and the weeds were three feet high. I pulled out my cloth measuring tape to double check and as I expected it was nearly 18 inches over city code. I called the city and the bank, complaining, but still no one came out. I might have to take matters into my own hands. I could feel Mrs. Hiro peeking out her front window at me. She must have been trying to figure out why I was measuring the grass. I put my measuring tape away back in my pocket and gave her a wave. She closed the curtains quickly. Some neighbors might think I'm a busybody and that I should mind my own business. I live here. This is my business.

The asphalt on the long driveway was cracking horribly. It should have been resealed last year. The whole house was an eyesore. I walked along, examining the cracking driveway which led to the detached two-car garage behind the bungalow. That's where I saw the postal truck idling. Strange, why would Gary pull into this driveway?

I peeked inside the open driver's cab. It was empty except for his cup of Starbuck's coffee. I touched it, it was still warm. I thought I better not go any further in case nature called and he had to make a quick stop. This would be his best choice. The grass in the back yard was worse than the front. You could hide a body back here and no one would ever know. 12:38 p.m. I sat on the bumper of the postal truck waiting for Gary to finish his business. I checked my watch again. 12:40 p.m. Out of the corner of my eye, I saw something move in the tall weeds. They parted. Sassy came out, carrying something in her mouth. "Sassy, you bad girl. Does Anne know you're out again?" I asked her.

Sassy stared at me. "All right, dear, let me see what you have." I bent down and tried to grab her. She dropped the package and ran off. I picked it up. It was a half-open Kibbles treat sample package wrapped in foil and addressed to Anne Hillstrom. "Why would Sassy carry that down the block?" I mused. I looked down the path of trampled weeds Sassy laid down. I followed the trail of letters, packages, junk mail and catalogs. At its end, a pair of size eight black Oxford work shoes pointed up to the sky like the Wicked Witch of the East from underneath a rusty wheelbarrow. I lifted the wheelbarrow. There was nothing I could do. Gary was gone. Now I knew why the postman is late.

# Chapter Two

I directed the EMTs to the body, to Gary. Police Chief Mark Krundel answered my speed dial and sent out the full force. I find it's always best to start at the top when you have a problem. Ambulances, fire trucks and police cars flocked to our normally quiet dead-end street. Dead-end street was an appropriate description for the matter at hand. Their sirens cut through the still afternoon air.

"Jan, are you all right?" Chief Krundel asked me coming up to where I was standing in front of the abandoned house. Now in his fifties, Chief Krundel started as a Woodland View Patrolman out of the academy and worked his way up through the ranks. He is a good cop, good neighbor and a friend. I first met him when I did a ride along twenty-five years ago. I helped launch the pilot Community Task Force. I was a young woman of fifty then, and my husband, Gino, didn't relish the fact that I could be in danger and even more so that I might be late with dinner. But we worked it out. Chief Krundel, Patrolman Krundel, at that time, was just months out of the Marines and very green. I gave him directions around town. The first ride along was at night and as always things were quiet. We stopped at Chubby's Drive-through for greasy cheeseburgers and fries. He was a handsome boy, no more than 175 pounds, which looked good on his five foot nine inch frame. You could tell he was in the Corps because every answer ended with, "Yes, ma'am," "No, Ma'am." Back then he kept a crew cut. I hold myself responsible for his Chubby's double cheeseburger habit. The double cheeseburger with Italian beef and mozzarella topping habit. Since that first night, Mark has kept Chubby's in business. Now as I stand here looking at him, I'm sure he's pushing three hundred pounds.

"Mark, I'm fine."

"Jan, tell me what happened?"

"I was doing my afternoon rounds, waiting to deliver the mail. Gary was late as usual. I walked down the block to see if I could get a glimpse of his truck. I stopped here to measure the grass. You know it's almost a foot higher than city ordinance allows. I've told you about this before, Mark."

"Jan, I know, we'll get on it. But can we get back to the postman?"

"Yes, Gary." I paused for a moment. "I found Sassy, Anne Hillstrom's cat. You know Anne, my neighbor on the north side? Her white Persian was in the weeds in the backyard here. She was carrying a package. This one here." I handed him the foil wrapped treats. "I followed her trail back through the weeds and found poor Gary sticking out from underneath the wheelbarrow."

"Besides Gary, did you see anything else unusual today? Where there strangers on the block? Was there anyone else around?"

In my head, I went through the day's events. Nothing out of the ordinary other than Michael was slightly late with the papers. "Mark, no, the street was empty." I shook my head. "I don't understand, who would want to kill Gary? He was our mailman and he's also a neighbor. He lives in the brown ranch." I knew Mark would know which house I was talking about. There was only one brown ranch on the block.

"Jan, there's going to be more questions. We will need you to come in and give a statement," Mark said. "Gary was a federal employee so the FBI will be involved." He started to turn back to the crime scene.

I stopped him. "Mark, what about the undelivered mail? Do you want me to take care of it?" I asked.

The police chief shook his head. "The postal police are on their way. Let them handle it," he said.

I watched the beehive of activity, standing guard over the crowd of neighbors who gathered on the street. They all had questions, questions I had no answers for. After the EMTs took Gary away, the police secured the scene with their yellow tape. I helped them disperse the neighbors, sending everyone home.

5:17 p.m. Valerie would be home soon. My son-in-law Bill was working late. My granddaughter, Meg and her son, Danny, would be home for dinner by now. With all the excitement, I hadn't taken anything out for dinner or had time to go the store. I examined my pantry for a quick meal and then remembered the cheese tortellini that I made at Easter and froze. Those could be cooked quickly in a pot of boiling water with a splash of salt. I heated olive oil, garlic, salt and pepper in a sauté pan. After I boiled the tortellini, I put them in the pan with a spoonful of the pot water. I grated some fresh Parmesan cheese on top.

I carried the bowl downstairs to the main house. Meg and Danny were sitting at the dining room table, working on homework together. I sat down next to them to watch. "Hey, Gran, can you stay with Danny for a couple minutes? I have a phone call to make for work," Meg said.

"Sure, Meg," I said. "Danny, what are you working on?"

"It's a book report on Percy Jackson."

"How's it going?" I remembered the book. We read it together before bedtime.

"I kind of cheated because we watched the movie."

I do that all the time I thought with our monthly book club. "How's everything going at school?"

Danny got quiet.

"What's wrong?"

"I don't want to talk about it."

I took his face in my hands. "Tell Gran Gran, what's going on?"

"There's this kid, Jimmy, in my class. He's like twice as big as me and when we play tag at recess you're supposed to tap people on the back. Every time he's it, he punches me really hard in the back."

"Have you told him to stop?"

Danny shook his head.

"Why not?"

"Gran, Gran, I told you he's twice my size."

"Danny, the thing with bullies is that they're usually big chickens. The reason they pick on smaller kids is because they're afraid to fight anyone their own size. They're afraid they're not good enough. They're not tough enough. The best fight to be in is the one where you just walk away. Next time he starts something with you, you walk away. If he follows you and he's going to hurt you, punch him right in the nose," I told him.

"Gran, Gran, I'll get in trouble," Danny said.

"I'm not saying start the fight. I'm not saying fighting is right, but you have to defend yourself. This world is full of bullies. There are good people, too, but you can't be afraid. OK?"

"Ok? Gran, Gran." Danny gave me a big hug.

"I want you to know I always have your back." I held him a moment too long. He pulled away.

Meg came back in the room, talking loudly on her cell phone. Valerie walked in the front door. "Ma, what happened today? I heard it on the news. I tried to call you. You didn't call me back," she said. She looked concerned; she was always worrying about me. It's funny I thought it should be the other way around. When do the kids become the parents? I guess it's all part of growing old. I'm sure she'll go through it one day with Meg. She came into the kitchen. When I look at her, I see myself at her age. At fifty years old, she is stunning. Her long dark hair with no signs of gray yet, her hazel eyes clear and bright, her olive skin free from wrinkles except the worry lines around her eyes. She is a worrier.

"Valerie, I've been too busy. I had to supervise traffic. There were news reporters, EMTs, the police. And I had to keep the neighbors from bothering them all," I said.

"Ma, you must have been scared." Valerie set her leather briefcase on the table.

My daughter knows me as mom, caregiver, cook. She doesn't know how many dead bodies I've seen. "Valerie, there's some pasta warming on the stove. I've got to get ready for Bunco." I stood up.

"Ma, you're not going out, are you?"

"It's Bunco night. Of course, I'm going. I'm in charge," I said, stopping to kiss Daniel and Meg before heading back upstairs.

I sprinkled powdered sugar on the Italian wedding cookies, a recipe passed down in my family for generations. The secret is you have to let them cool off after you take them out of the fryer. Then you can add the powered sugar. Otherwise it gets all goopy. It was my night to bring snacks, and I always say homemade is best made.

## Chapter Three

Woodland View's VFW hall is the family room of the community. Everything takes place here from Boy Scout pancake breakfasts to church spaghetti dinners. And, once a month our community Bunco game. I arrived at the VFW hall to find North Linden Avenue Jan taking over, setting up the tables for the night's game. She was doing it all wrong. I knew there would be no avoiding the conversation. "Jan, how are you?" I asked.

"Fine, Jan. How are you?" She stood tall, her lanky frame and the lines on her face made her look like a wooden ruler. She doesn't have the natural curves that I have. Maybe that was part of her problem with me. The boys always preferred me to her. "I heard the terrible news about South Linden this afternoon. How horrifying for you and your block," she said. "I walked over but you looked busy."

"Yes, it's a tragedy but we have everything under control. Chief Krundel is on top of things. I'm helping with the investigation."

"I'm sure he appreciates all your help," Jan said in a snide voice.

"Listen, I have to put these cookies down and organize the

tables."

"Wedding cookies, how nice. They were good the last time you brought them." North Linden Avenue Jan never bothers hiding her sarcasm.

Setting the cookies down on the long table in the back, I straightened the eight card tables that the other Jan lined up incorrectly. I placed the pads of paper, pens and dice on the tables. I then set up the head table for myself and my co-captain Helen. She lives in the yellow split level with Jake, the yellow corgi. Jake and I have an understanding like Sassy and I do. We keep a polite distance from each other.

The tables filled up quickly. It was a busy night. Eight tables of four chairs, everyone filled. Thirty-one ladies and one gentleman, James, 65, never married. Some of the widows showed interest but I think these ladies are not James' cup of tea, James is very sophisticated and elegant, I'm sure his taste in women runs the same way. The Bunco ladies are wonderful and sweet, but they don't travel in the same social circles that James travels. Most of his friends that I have met are professors he worked with at the university, or actors from the community theater where James volunteers. His close friend Roger was a professional dancer of some sort, James told me they met at a dance. James lives across the street from me. He keeps his brick colonial immaculate inside and out.

In the old days, the room would have been thick with smoke from Lady Pall Malls but smoking's outlawed everywhere nowadays. It took me thirty years to quit so I don't miss it now. The room grew loud with the clatter of dice against the card tables. There was also the nonstop chatter of voices. For those of you unfamiliar with the proper way to play Bunco, it's really easy. There are six rounds of play. The first round you roll the dice hoping to get as many ones as you can. You keep rolling until you don't roll a one. Then the next player goes until they stop rolling ones. And, so on, until the head table reaches 21. Then the losers rotate to the next table. And, then everyone rolls for twos. And, so on, and so on. A bit more challenging than my Friday night bingo.

Our group takes a fifteen-minute break between the two games. I stood by the snack table, making sure everyone had enough cookies and coffee. James came up to me. Out of everyone here, he is the one I most enjoyed talking to. Since he moved onto the block ten years ago, he has become a dear and trusted friend.

"Jan, tell me what happened," James said as he bit into one of my cookies. "Delicious by the way. You waited with the powdered sugar, didn't you?"

"Yes, James, that was a good tip. Thank you very much."

"I've never felt unsafe on our block before. Nothing bad ever happens. Well, last summer we had the high school kids drinking in the woods at the end of the block. Nothing this terrible. This a murder, on South Linden, I can't believe it." James shuddered.

"Poor Gary. Thank God he was single and didn't leave a family behind," I said.

"You, Jan, what about you? You found him. That must have been frightening."

I found James' voice very soothing. Almost melodic. I knew he was concerned, he is a very sincere man. "Police Chief Krundel has everything under control. South Linden is still the safest block in DuPage County. We watch out for our own."

"You know, Jan, this is like a chapter out of one of our mystery lovers book club selections," James said. "I hate to make light of a tragedy but what a story."

Some story, I thought.

Helen rang the bell that signaled the start of game two. I took my position at the head table. I'd been on a winning streak so I had stayed at the head table all night. When game two was finished, we added up everyone's scores. Cash prizes were given to the highest scorer; the low scorer received a consolation prize and was responsible for bringing treats to the next game. I left with my winnings, $25. Not bad for a night's work.

James offered to drive me home but I enjoy walking. The spring night was cool and refreshing. The woods along Woodland View Road came alive with the sounds of the forest waking up. An eight-point buck stood on the road, staring me down. I shooed him off back into the woods. I have no understanding with the deer, raccoons or skunks. I expect them to keep their distance. I keep mine. It's better that way.

I could hear thunder rolling in from the west. I quickened my pace. Lightning exploded over the golf course that backs up to Woodland View Road. A drizzle started and turned into an out and out downpour. I should have taken James up on his offer. I was soaked, my Keds squished with each step. I turned onto Spring Oaks, making my way down to Linden Avenue. By the time I reached Linden Avenue, the street was a river. I sloshed my way through it, the water clear up to my knees in parts. I stopped to help my neighbor unclog the drain in front of her house but there was nowhere for the water to go. I saw another neighbor struggling to recover her child's Big Wheel that was floating downhill to the end of the block into the woods. I helped her secure it.

When I got to my house, I found Valerie and Bill in the basement sopping up the backed-up sewer. At some point on Linden Avenue when the rains are this bad, we give up and let the basement go. Valerie has learned over the years that it's inevitable the basement will flood. She replaced the laminated wood floor with tile. Everyone on South Linden Avenue has learned to waterproof their basement with tile, outdoor rugs and greenboard.

As fast as the rain came, it left. Nine and a half inches fell in an hour. I went outside to survey the damage to my street. The river was turning into a stream. City workers drove up and down the street passing sandbags out to neighbors who needed them. I called our Mayor and the head of streets and sanitation. No one could make it out. There'd be nothing for them to do anyway. After countless surveys and city meetings, the Woodland View officials blamed God. My answer was I'm not Noah, and this ain't the Bible.

I helped neighbors carry out water-damaged rugs and furniture from their water logged basements. By the time I made it home it was after 1 a.m., and I was exhausted.

Vicki Vass

## Chapter Four

Next morning, the sun was out like nothing happened the night before. The street was dry, but the curb showed the remnants of the damage from the storm. I gathered the fallen tree branches from the sidewalk as I walked to the end of the block. I waited for our garbage man, Peter. When I saw his truck, I waved him down. He was hanging off the back of the Woodland View Streets and Sanitation truck. He motioned for Dave to stop and jumped off the back.

"Hi Grandma Jan, we're on time this week even with the storm," Peter said.

"Morning, Peter. I wanted to warn you that the Andersons have a lot of heavy, wet rugs and furniture on their curb from the flood last night. I helped them cut the rugs up and bind them. I tried to hammer down all the nails from the paneling but be careful," I told him.

"Thanks, Grandma Jan, I appreciate the warning. I'll be careful," he said.

"You take care now," I said. Oh no, out of the corner of my eye, coming briskly at me was North Linden Avenue Jan accompanied by her know-it-all daughter, Celia. She was coming to survey our damage and gloat on our misfortune. She stopped when she reached the north curb of Spring Oaks, the dividing line between North and South Linden Avenue, I stood silent on the south curb. The street was a neutral zone. The DMZ (demilitarized zone) separating two opposing forces.

She waved and yelled, "Jan." She ran towards me.

My left eye twinged a bit.

"Jan," North Linden Avenue Jan said. "I surveyed my block last night, checking out the storm damage. We did all right, not too much water. What about your block? Did you have a lot of damage?"

North Linden Avenue Jan knows quite well that South Linden Avenue rests at the bottom of the slight hill causing all of their rainwater to drain down to our drains at the end of the block. We get a lot of North Linden Avenue's problems. I'm standing in front of one of them right now. "Nothing we can't handle. It's the rainy season. Once a year we know we're getting hit hard. Everything's been cleaned up. Appreciate your concern," I said.

"Has the mayor been out to look around?" North Linden Avenue Jan asked.

"Not yet. I called him last night. There's nothing to see," I said. "Wait, there's Helen, I have to go talk to her. I'll see you at the meeting." I walked over to Helen, who was walking Jake the corgi.

"Helen, how'd you do last night?" I asked, turning my back to North Linden Avenue Jan and her daughter. I watched them walk down the street, inspecting all the water soaked furniture and rugs tossed at the curb faster than Peter could dispose of them.

"It's a mess. The rainwater is not so bad but I'm still cleaning the sewer backup in my laundry room. Thanks to your advice the stone tile floor I installed cleans up much easier than the linoleum."

"It looks more high end, don't you think," I said, not waiting for a response. "Helen, don't forget the emergency city council meeting tonight. We need everybody to attend so we can talk about how to fix the flooding problem."

"I'll be there. Believe me. I've got a few words for the city council," Helen said.

I walked with Helen all the way to the dog park, which was less than a mile away. The park district built the off-leash park on the edge of the forest preserve on Woodland View Road, the main road running through the center of town. The air was fresh and clean after the rain. It was a beautiful spring day, and the dogs were enjoying the weather as much as I was. Split into two sections, German Shepherds and Labradors chased each other around the largest area of the park. I personally think the two sections are dedicated to separate the smart dogs from the big happy dogs. Most of the big happy hunting dogs were on one side chasing balls and sniffing them. On the other side were the border collies and herding dogs. They always seem more intense. When they look at me, I feel like they can read my mind. It makes me uncomfortable. Sprinkled in were little dogs, mutts and terriers who seemed happy to be out on this nice day.

When Helen went inside the park with Jake, I saw my neighbor Monika. She was leaving with Boo Boo, her Australian shepherd. Out of all the herding dogs in the park, the Australian shepherd strikes me as the most intelligent. Something in their eyes holds my attention. I think if I were a dog lover that would be the breed I would have. I think I appreciate them, too, because they are a working dog and I appreciate a good day's work. I walked home with Monika, chatting about the flood. As we passed by Mr. Hiro's house, I could see the curtain was parted. It was Mrs. Hiro. I waved at her. She closed the curtain quickly. I continued walking with Monika.

## Chapter Five

I pulled up at the Woodland View Police Station. It is a modern two-story facility attached to the city hall. Both were built during the housing boom in the early 2000s. As I opened the large glass door, Carol from Community Service was walking out. Seeing her reminded me that I meant to call her weeks ago. The annual police National Night Out was coming up in a few weeks. I thought it would be a good opportunity to catch her before she headed out to check the commuter lot for parking violators.

Her red curly hair poked out from under her blue service cap. Her uniform fit snugly around her curves. A single mom in her forties, I couldn't figure out why she was still single. I asked James if maybe some of his younger friends might be interested in her. None of them had girlfriends so they were all available. James promised to look into it but he never got back to me. I would remind him again. "Hi, Jan," she said.

"Hi Carol. Do you have a minute? I wanted to talk to you about plans for the night out," I said, holding the door open for her.

She smiled at me. "Sure. How about we sit over on the bench? I have a few minutes." We walked over to one of the wood benches scattered around the courtyard of the police station. It was a nice place to sit and have a cup of coffee. Over the past few weeks, the city workers planted white and red impatiens around the green area of the courtyard. Hanging baskets containing flowing petunias draped down over the side of the lampposts. I stared at the streetlight. I can't tell you how many times I've called the city about our block and streetlights; we don't have any. Of course, the ones installed here are the expensive streetlights, the fancy ones that look like old-fashioned coach lights. All the city buildings have the nice streetlights. The residential areas have the no-frills kind.

"Carol, last year we ordered pizza, we watched movies, played dodge ball, basketball. It was fun. I was wondering if we could try something new this year?" I asked.

"What'd you have in mind?" Carol asked, putting on her mirrored sunglasses.

"James suggested that we either play old-fashioned charades or have the kids do a talent show. James said he could ask some his friends from the community theater group to help out, and that he would be glad to help organize it."

Carol's face went blank. I couldn't tell if she didn't like the idea or if she was thinking. "Oh, Jan, we're going to have fifty to sixty eight- and nine-year-olds drinking soda, all hyped on sugar running around a gym. I don't know if they're going to want to sit still to watch a talent show. That's why we do the physical activities to tire them out."

"That's kind of what I told James but he feels that the kids especially at this age should be exposed to more art, get them away from their iPods, iPads, iPhones or whatever else they have. Maybe we could make it like America's has talent. We could call it Woodland View has talent and talk to the local merchants about prizes."

"Jan, it sounds like it could be fun especially if James is involved. Let me talk to the chief," Carol said.

"I'll mention it to him. I'm on my way to see him. I will let you go." I stood up.

"Jan, we'll talk again. I'll see you at bingo." I watched Carol walk away. I really wish I could help her find a nice young man. I would mention it to James again.

As I was heading back toward the building, I noticed some weeds sprouting between the impatiens. I pulled them out and deposited them in the garbage can. I put my hands on my hip and did a 360 looking out onto the courtyard. I was pleased with the work they had done. I went back inside. Chief Krundel was waiting for me at the front desk. He pulled me into his office. He closed the door and shut the blinds of the glass window that looked into his office. "Jan, sit down, I want to talk to you before Agent Peabody gets here," he said.

"Sure, Chief, what do you want to talk about?"

Mark walked around behind his desk and squeezed into his armchair. The wooden chair creaked a bit. It made me concerned both for him and the chair. "Jan, you and I go way back, and we have an understanding. A relationship wouldn't you say?"

"Hmm, of course, Mark."

"I tend to give you a lot of leeway with police matters. I know that you have the best interest of the city at heart always but the FBI is a different matter. They're not going to cut you that kind of slack."

"Mark, what are you talking about?"

"What I'm saying, Jan, is that this is an official murder investigation. You're a civilian. You have to stand behind the ropes. Do you know what I mean? You have to watch what you say and what you do around the FBI."

Mark and I have known each other for a long time. I respect him, and we do have a relationship. He has no idea who I was before I came to Woodland View. I've dealt with the FBI before. People see us for who they think we are. Mark only knows the Woodland View version of me. "Mark, I understand what you're saying. The last thing I want to do is step on any toes."

"Good, Jan, we understand each other then?" he said. I nodded in agreement.

"I spoke with Carol about the national night out next month. We're talking about having a talent show. James has volunteered to help organize it and help with the music."

"He has, has he?" the chief asked.

"And, Mark, by the way, James is hosting hot yoga classes at his house every Sunday. I think that you would enjoy it. I've been to a couple. It's fun."

"Hot yoga, really?"

"It's just a thought," I said.

There was a timid knock on the door. "Come in," Chief Krundel said. The door slowly opened, and the young FBI agent came in, flashing his badge, and introducing himself as Agent Peabody. The agent was very handsome. His dark curly hair was cut short which was appropriate; his steel blue eyes were alert. His chiseled face reminded me of a young Tom Cruise, Tom Cruise from Top Gun not Mission Impossible Tom Cruise. Not that that's a bad thing. I could tell right away he was fresh out of Quantico. His navy blue suit still had a price tag peeking out from under the back of his collar.

I had foregone my daily activities to meet him at the Woodland View Police Department. He offered to come to my house to see me but I wanted to save him the trouble. After the introductions, Chief Krundel said, "You can use my office." He grabbed his coffee cup and left the room.

"New to the service?" I asked.

"How could you tell?" Agent Peabody appeared surprised at my question.

I reached around the back of his neck and pulled off the price tag. I handed it to him.

Crumpling it in his pocket, his face turned red. "Mrs. Kustodia."

I interrupted him, "Jan. Call me Jan."

I watched as Agent Peabody sat down across from me in Chief Krundel's seat. The agent sat on an angle and gave me a big smile. He tilted his head as he spoke, "I wanted to review the events of the day starting with when you discovered Gary Ingall."

I sat back and reflected before speaking. I wanted to make sure I remembered everything clearly. "Gary was late with the mail so I walked down the block to see if I could see his truck. He usually delivers mail to North Linden Avenue first. It's closer to the post office. As I got to the abandoned house, the foreclosure, I noticed the cracks in the blacktopped driveway were getting worse. I called the city and complained several times but they always told me they're not responsible. I followed the cracks back behind the house. That's when I saw his truck by the garage."

"And then what happened?" Agent Peabody prompted me, raising his eyebrows and smiling at me.

"I looked inside the truck and Gary wasn't there. I thought maybe he had to do his business, you know what I mean. Gary is, I mean was, very lazy. And if nature called, I think Gary would take the easiest route to answer." I paused. "I waited for a while and that's when I saw my neighbor's cat coming out of the weeds, carrying a package. I thought that was unusual. She's a housecat. Then I noticed the mail lying on the ground. I followed it and found Gary." The door opened, and I smiled at Chief Krundel as he brought me another cup of coffee. He made it just like I liked, black and strong. Agent Peabody gave the chief a pointed glance towards his empty coffee cup. Chief Krundel left the room, closing the door behind him.

Agent Peabody shifted in his chair so he was facing me dead on. I glanced over at his hands. When we first started talking, his hands were facing up. Now they were facing down. He was trying to read my body language as much as I was reading his. I hadn't given him any tell yet because there was nothing for me to hide. Everything I was telling him as far as I knew was true. I smiled and tilted my head to match the angle of his. His hands flipped back up, a sign that he was open to what I was saying. He believed me. The best lie detecting machine can be tricked but the human body always has a tell. Agent Peabody and I understood and trusted each other. We had silently made that agreement. "Did you see anything suspicious? Did you see anyone around the house? Or some one you didn't recognize?" Agent Peabody asked.

"No, at the time I was the only one out. I remember thinking how quiet our street was," I said. "At that time of day, most everyone else is at work. I did see Mr. Hiro in the morning working in his garden."

"Mr. Hiro?" Agent Peabody scribbled in his notepad.

"Yes, he lives in the house next to the abandoned house where I found Gary. Koji Hiro. I think he's a contractor or he might be retired. He's always working on his driveway and his garden."

"Koji. That's K O J I."

"Yes, that's right." I continued. "We nodded at each other earlier while I was talking with Mike."

"Mike?"

"Mike Henderson. He delivers our newspapers."

Agent Peabody jotted down Mike's name. "I understand you've lived in Woodland View for forty years. You must know everybody on the block. Has Mr. Hiro lived on South Linden very long?"

I thought for a moment and I couldn't remember when they moved in. Mr. and Mrs. Hiro are always so quiet and keep to themselves. "Two, three years ago at the most."

Agent Peabody continued scribbling in his notebook. He had very fine penmanship. The FBI agents I had known in the past had chicken scratch writing. It was hard for me to decipher their notes upside down. I could read Agent Peabody's with no problem.

"How was Gary killed?" I asked him.

The agent sat back in the wooden chair, stretching his fingers out. "The case is currently under investigation. We're not allowed to give out any information."

A long time ago, I learned that what people say and what they write are two different things. I saw him start writing something next to Gary's name. As we spoke, there was a tap on the office window, which distracted him. He never finished. It was Chief Krundel trying to get his attention. Agent Peabody excused himself and stepped out carrying his notepad.

When he returned, he was carrying a coffee mug. He sat back down and opened his notepad again.

"Is this your first assignment?" I asked.

"I'm temporarily assigned to the Chicago bureau."

"So, this is your first assignment. I think you're doing a fine job. I'll be sure to let Deputy Director Claypool know."

"How do you know the Deputy Director?"

"We're old friends," I said.

He hesitated for a moment. I could tell he wanted to ask more questions about my relationship with the deputy director. I don't like to name drop but I thought it might put the young agent at ease knowing that I was friends with his boss' boss and that I would put a good word in for him. He thought better of asking and said, "Thank you, Mrs. Kustodia, Jan. If I have any further questions, I know how to contact you." He closed his notebook.

I stood up and walked toward the door. Chief Krundel stood there, waiting to escort me to my car. "Thanks for coming in, Jan," he said. "I'll see you at the council meeting."

We walked outside to my car. "Oh, Mark, let me know if you want James to move forward with his talent show idea, and don't forget Sunday at 2 p.m. hot yoga," I said, opening my car door.

## Chapter Six

I stood in James' gourmet kitchen. It is gorgeous, it is his masterpiece. It took him years to design and he labored over every detail. The brown-speckled granite countertop was flown in direct from Italy. The 10-foot long island slab took six men to carry it into the house. I should know, I supervised the installation. Like everything James does, it always has to be the best. The kitchen could be in one of those fancy home magazines with its Viking stove and Sub-Zero refrigerator. Not sure why he needs all that, I manage well enough on my Sears gas stove and Kenmore refrigerator. The stove gets stuff hot and the refrigerator keeps stuff cold. What else do you need?

Today we're preparing for book club. I came over early to help James. As always, James has an elaborate plan. His flare for dramatics is fun. I enjoy his company, and he is a wonderful cook. I don't mind helping him out.

James came back into the kitchen, carrying bottles of wine from his basement wine cellar. Another extravagance that could be in one of those home magazines. I was fine with my gallon jug of Gallo.

"Jan, this is going to be the best book club ever." James was wearing freshly pressed designer jeans, a cashmere sweater and hiking boots. I couldn't imagine what the game plan was.

"I'm not sure you can top the tour of the Frank Lloyd Wright studio," I said. We toured the home of the famous architect but I couldn't recall the name of the book.

"*Loving Frank*," he said as if he read my mind.

"Yeah, *Loving Frank*. I thought it was about Frank Sinatra. That's why I started reading it." My Frank, Frank Sinatra, wouldn't have liked the book either.

"You never finish any of the books," he said. "In fact, I don't even think you pick them up."

"I come for the atmosphere. When we read *Julie and Julia*,"

"Were supposed to read," he interrupted me.

"I didn't need to read it. I saw the movie with Meg. Meryl Streep was wonderful," I said. "Having the book club at Le Titi di Paris was a great idea. The food was delicious." I sat back, recalling the beef bourguignon. James asked the chef to prepare it especially for our club. James knew a lot of people and he knew how to get things done.

"Tonight, Jan, is very special. I'm sure if you read the book." James picked up his copy of the book. I read the title quickly. It was *In the Woods* by Tana French. "I've picked the perfect spot to discuss this murder mystery."

"What's it about, James?"

"Oh, Jan, you're kidding me, right?" He turned over the back cover and read, "In Tana French's powerful debut thriller, three children leave their small Dublin neighborhood to play in the surrounding woods."

"So, you're telling me we're having book club in the woods. Is that what's happening?"

"Of course, it's a murder mystery, my favorite. What better place to discuss a murder that happens in the woods than in the woods." He paused. "We can walk right out my back door and enjoy a picnic lunch in the clearing a couple hundred feet from here. I've already scoped out the area. It's perfect. There is a blanket of wildflowers blooming already."

"We're going to sit on the ground. Is it damp?" I asked.

"No, it's dry, Jan. I put a blanket down with a tarp underneath to make it extra cozy. Isn't it fun?" James asked.

I knew better than to try to talk James out of his plan. He was smiling his perfect James smile, his turquoise contacts glistened. I thought we could certainly discuss the book sitting on his back deck looking out at the woods. But James was a purist. If the book was set in the woods then James would be in the woods. Next month's book title was *Sin in the Second City*, I couldn't image what theme location James would dream up for that meeting.

James pulled things out of his fridge, piling them onto the island. "To keep with the theme, the entire menu features traditional Irish picnic food. We're starting with Kerrygold cheese from Ireland. I've got cheddar, Emmental and Dubliner. To accompany the cheese, we have an Irish fruit chutney of apple and pear. I made it myself. And, of course, we have Branson pickles. They're sour. It will cut through the sweetness. Water crackers and soda bread."

As James named the foods off, my head grew dizzy. His hands flew around the kitchen like he was directing an orchestra. He was very worked up. He got worked up over good books and good food.

"I also have a nice red wine and for those who dare an Irish whiskey." He added the two bottles to the growing pile by the picnic basket.

"That sounds great."

"Wait, Jan, I'm not done. For the main course, I made bridies. It's a meat pie. It can be eaten hot or cold. Perfect for a picnic." He organized items into a large wicker picnic basket. "And, I've made an Irish whiskey cake. The lemon cake is tart and sweet, a perfect complement to the whiskey."

"Boy, that almost makes me want to read the book, James," I said.

"You're bad, Jan." He packed everything into the baskets. As he finished, I skimmed through the book. I needed a general idea for the discussion. It didn't hold my interest. I peeked out his kitchen garden window through his collection of herbs and spices that grow in antique pots. I couldn't remember what the pots were called. James knows every antique in his house, when it was made and where he found it.

We gathered in the backyard. James told everyone to meet there. Over the past few years, James turned his backyard into an English rose garden complete with a fieldstone fence wall that surrounded the large double lot. His back deck is made of slate with a little walkway leading through the patches of English roses. James already told us that he wants to host the August mystery lover's book meeting. The book title escapes me, it probably has to do with a garden murder or flowers. I'd get to it eventually. No, let's be honest, probably not.

We walked along the little path. There were seven of us in all. Helen, her daughter, Sandy, who moved back after graduating from Iowa State with her MBA. My old friend Marian from the library. Monika. And, Helen invited North Linden Jan. Helen lives on the border between the two Linden Avenues. She always feels obligated to include North Linden Jan.

James opened the wrought iron gate that led out into the woods. It swung open with a creak. He turned around and smiled at me. "OOOH, Spooky." Then he told the others, "I had my gardener mow a path to the clearing."

It was an easy walk, no more than a couple hundred yards. The elm trees that bordered the backyards gave way to old growth oak trees, the heart of the DuPage County Forest. Their canopy with the new leaves hovered over us blocking the sun until we reached the clearing. The April showers did bring May flowers. The little meadow was filled with purple sage, Irises and crocus. It was actually quite lovely.

James had placed a blanket large enough for all of us to sit. I sat down slowly, hoping I would be able to get back up from the ground. I wasn't what you'd call outdoorsy. My husband, Gino, and I traveled the country in a RV one year. We saw all the sights; the Grand Canyon and Mount Rushmore but we either stayed in the RV or a hotel. That was my idea of roughing it.

James opened and poured the wine. The cheese was set out and we all helped ourselves. I listened to the conversation about the book, not joining in. When they got to the part of the story where the dead body was found, James stopped and everyone looked over at me. I had only been half listening. When I looked up from eating my piece of cheese I was surprised to see everyone staring at me. "What? What'd I miss?"

"Jan, this isn't upsetting you, is it?" Helen asked.

"What do you mean?" I asked back.

"The dead body. I mean after you know, Gary," Helen said.

"Oh, Gary. I'm fine." I hoped my words would assure her.

"Do you want to talk about it?" Helen asked.

I felt like I was at one of those interventions. I'd seen them on those reality shows that Meg watches. They never end well, and I didn't believe they were so real either. "There's really nothing to talk about. The police are investigating. I'm confident that Chief Krundel will find out what happened to Gary."

"That was only three houses away from me. What if it was me? What if it was my daughter? I've never been worried about our safety in this neighborhood until now," Helen said. "I can't believe you're not upset."

I looked around at the faces of my dear friends, my neighbors. I felt like I couldn't find the words to comfort them, to ease their fears. They were worried about me and for themselves. "I am upset, Helen. I'm angry but I'm not afraid." I had seen worse. I don't normally talk about the war, that's behind me now. "I was one of the last surgical nurses in Saigon in 1975 before the Army evacuated. The boys that were left behind to cover our backs were hit hard by the Viet Cong. It was me and two other nurses. Gino was the only surgeon. He wouldn't leave without me and I wouldn't leave until all the soldiers were out of there," I said. "I've seen the worst of what humans can do to each other, and at some point it makes you numb. You have to feel that way to go on. It's the only way to survive." I stared out at their nervous faces. I needed to reassure them that I was ok and that they would be safe. "Look, everyone, life goes on. This was a tragedy but we've got each other's backs. We watch out for our own. We're safe because we have each other."

The conversation returned to the book. I think my words comforted them in some way. While the others were talking, North Linden Jan came and sat down next to me. "Are you planning to go to the city council meeting?" North Linden Jan asked me.

"I haven't missed a meeting in forty years. Why would you think I'd missed this one?"

"You've had a lot going on," North Linden Jan said. "I went door to door to make sure everyone was coming. I think it's important you do the same for your block."

I was getting upset now with NLJ. Nobody told me how to conduct business on my street. I had to get some air before I said something I might regret. "Excuse me, Jan," I said. My knees creaked as I uncrossed my legs to get up from the ground. I walked over to the edge of the field to look at the Irises. I bent down to smell the sage. It smelled horrible. Or, something smelled rotten. I walked further into the woods and I found the source of the smell. It smelled like what it was -- death. I swatted the flies that were buzzing around me. And, then I found the rotting big bullfrog. It was covered in maggots. When I got back to the others, James was serving the meat pie.

## Chapter Seven

After picking Danny up from the bus stop, I sat on the front porch, sipping my afternoon tea. He was playing street hockey with his friends in front of our house. I told Meg I would watch him while she went shopping. From my rocking chair, I could see Mr. Hiro out in his front garden, flashes of purple peeked through his evergreens as Mrs. Hiro fluttered about wearing her purple silk kimono. It was late afternoon and warm for spring. Valerie's tulips were starting to break through the mulch. The crocuses and daffodils were already in bloom. The Anderson's weeping cherry tree was awash with pink and white blossoms.

Directly across from our house is the split rail fence that divides South Linden from the DuPage County Forest Preserve. It doesn't do much to stop the deer from jumping over or the raccoons from crawling under. I have a slight tolerance for the deer but the raccoons try my patience. The little sneak thieves. They knocked over the garbage cans and refused to clean up after themselves.

Mr. Hiro finished his weeding and got into his white panel van. He took off. I always thought it was a bit unusual that his work van has no name on it. Most contractors I've seen on the block have their company logo or phone number on their van. In fact, I wasn't even sure what kind of contract work he did. I've seen ladders on top of his van. A few times I've noticed him carrying duffel bags and tools from his back yard to the van. I guess I assumed that he worked in construction.

Meg's gray Lincoln Navigator pulled into the driveway. It was a little flashy for my taste but these young folks are all about status symbols these days with their designer names. iPhones. Uggs. North Face. Prada. Where I grew up on Taylor Street in Chicago, the only labels we were concerned about were the ones we placed on each other.

"Hi Meg." I ran down to help her unload the groceries from the back of the SUV.

Throwing his stick on the ground, Danny ran up, gave me a hug. "Gran, Gran, did you see me? Did you see that goal?"

"Yes, Danny," I said turning around to give him an encouraging smile. "You're really good."

"Are you coming to my hockey game on Saturday?" He grabbed one of the bags from my hand.

"Of course, I wouldn't miss it." I could never say no to him. I held back the urge to pinch his little round face. It is an Italian custom reserved for grandmothers, and in my case an Italian great-grandmother. Danny didn't care for it especially in front of his friends.

I watched him go into the house, carrying his bags of groceries. I followed him with the few remaining bags. Danny set his bags down on the granite island and went back towards the door. "Danny," Meg said. "Grab your guitar. I want you to practice your lesson before dinner."

"C'mon, Mom, they're still playing hockey in front," Danny argued. "Can I practice later?"

"Danny, now, before dinner," Meg said in her stern mom voice. She constantly impressed me. I watched her grow from a scared young twenty-year-old single mother to a confident, successful mortgage broker and wonderful mother.

"Go get your guitar," I said to Danny. "I'll sit with you on the front porch. I want to catch up with your mom first." Danny left the room. I heard the screen door slam behind him a few minutes later. "How was work today?" I asked Meg as she put the groceries away.

"Good, Gran. Busy, I processed several loans, the market is picking up." Meg reached up in the pantry to store the reusable grocery bags. "I wanted to talk to you. I have to fly to Ohio for a couple days next month for a mortgage broker's seminar. Can you help watch Danny?"

"Is that the same weekend as the police night out?" I asked. I was always ready to help Meg, and I enjoyed spending time with Danny.

"Yes, will that be OK?"

"Of course, Danny could sleep at my place after the night out. He can even invite his hockey buddies."

"Gran, he's been talking about doing an overnight in the tree house," Meg said. Bill and Danny did a project together every year, a way for just the guys to hang out. Usually it was related to hockey or

Cub Scouts. Last year it was building a tree house in the hundred foot tall oak bordering our back fence. From the tree house, you can look out into the woods. It's the perfect venue for ghost stories. I've climbed up the tree house with Danny several times but we've never spent an entire night.

"Meg, that sounds like fun." I looked around the kitchen; everything was now in its proper place. I trained her well. "I'm going to go back outside," I said, exiting the house through the screen door. I sat on the porch, next to Danny who was plucking at the strings on the acoustic guitar, struggling with a song. "What song are you playing?" I asked.

"It's called *Raindrops keep falling on my head*. It's really lame," Danny said.

I didn't agree with him. I remembered the first time I heard the song. I was at the movie theater with Gino for the premiere of *Butch Cassidy and the Sundance Kid*. "Danny, you have to arch your wrist a little more. That's why you're getting the buzzing sound on the strings," I said.

"Gran, Gran, I can't do it. My hands don't bend like that," he said.

"Danny, it takes time and practice."

He put the guitar down, frustrated. I picked it up and played *Innamorata*.

Danny's eyes opened wide. "Gran, Gran, I didn't know you played guitar."

I stopped. "Years of practice, Danny." I played the rest of the song, singing along. "If our lips should meet, innamorata. Kiss me, kiss me sweet, innamorata."

Danny stopped me. "What does that word mean?"

"Honey, it's Italian for my love. It was your great-grandfather and mine's wedding song. We were working at the Sabre Room, a restaurant in Chicago, and the man who sings that song, Dean Martin, was playing there. He was very famous. He sat me down at a table before the show and sang it to me."

"Why, Gran Gran?"

I thought for a moment about how to put it into words appropriate for an eight-year-old. "He wanted to be my friend. When your great-grandfather Gino saw Dean Martin singing to me, he came over, grabbed my hand, pulled me in his arms and we danced while Dean Martin sang that song. That's the night I knew I was going to marry him."

"That's nice. Dean Martin sounds cool."

"Yes, he was very cool." I said, handing Danny the guitar back. "Practice, I'm going for a walk." I ruffled his hair. I could hear the strained notes of Raindrops falling off the porch as I stepped onto the sidewalk. I could have turned right and walked down to the end of block. The street ended at the forest preserve, and it was pretty at this time of the evening. Instinctively I turned left, heading north up Linden Avenue. I found myself standing in front of Mr. Hiro's house.

I tiptoed around his half-finished driveway. If he was a contractor, he sure was taking a long time finishing it. There was one finished slab, just big enough to park his van. This was a work in progress since he moved in. Yes, it was two years ago, I remembered now. It was the summer the streets were all torn up. That's when he started building his driveway. Nobody could park on the street that summer.

I crept around the back of his little pillbox ranch. In all my years on this block, I have never been past the front yard. The back was hidden by tall evergreens. I slipped past them and entered the side yard, which he shared with the abandoned house. I followed the stone walkway around to the back and stopped. It was the last house on the block, which gave it a massive yard on both sides separating it from its neighbors.

The split rail fence that separated the yard from the forest was torn down. I stared at the yard, the stone path wound around a sand Zen garden. I felt like I was in the garden of Kyoto. My husband, Gino, was stationed by Mount Fuji after the Vietnam War. When we lived there, we visited the Zen gardens. I found them very peaceful and calming. Mr. Hiro's crushed gravel and sand Zen garden was just as beautiful and peaceful. It bordered the huge koi pond.

I walked over the sandalwood bridge that expanded over the length of that 30-foot wide koi pond. The koi must have felt my footsteps. They all splashed around the bridge like it was feeding time. His white cherry blossom trees were in bloom, the scent was intoxicating. On the small landing that jetted out into the pond, a cement Buddha sat, keeping watch. I felt like I had left the country. It was a secret world.

In the back corner was a large 10 X 10 foot cedar shed. Like the driveway, it must be on Mr. Hiro's to do list. The roof was sagging, the panels were cracked and popping off but the expensive steel padlock that sealed the door was new. It didn't make sense to me. It made me even more curious to see inside. I stood on my tiptoes to peek through one of the cracks.

"May I help you?" I heard a thickly accented voice from behind me.

I turned around. The voice belonged to Mr. Hiro. He stood in front of me, holding a rake. Mrs. Hiro was standing behind him. Despite his five-foot stature, his presence was intimidating as he towered over Mrs. Hiro. I did a quick recovery. "Mr. Hiro, I was searching for Anne Hillstrom's cat. She snuck out again. You know the white cat, have you seen her?"

He stood silent. I was reminded of Grant Wood's famous painting, American Gothic. I had seen it at the Chicago Art Institute, another one of James' book club trips. A monarch butterfly landed on top of his rake. It did not break his silence. Then he spoke in Japanese to Mrs. Hiro.

She answered him and bowed politely.

He returned his gaze to me and said, "We have not seen a cat."

"Thank you," I said. And then I did the most stupid thing I could do. I bowed like I was in a bad *Karate Kid* movie. Then I backed away and headed home.

## Chapter Eight

I made it to city hall right before the rain started. Living in Woodland View, we constantly check the skies in spring. My street bears the brunt of the rain water run off from the surrounding forest. Linden Avenue is a peninsula surrounded by the DuPage County Forest Preserve. To make matters worse two summers ago the city tore up South Linden to replace the sixty-year-old sewage pipes. We hoped it would solve the problem but it only added to it. Now the sewers backed up into our basements during the heaviest rains.

Over the past few years, the city contracted engineering consultants to find the source of the flooding problem and come up with a solution. Flood control is the topic of tonight's meeting.

Throughout the day, I knocked on my neighbors' doors encouraging them to attend tonight's meeting. I have found many Woodland View residents don't attend city council meetings. I don't understand that. I want to know what's going on. I make it a point to appear at every single one, whether or not I have something to say. And, especially this one that has such a direct impact on my street.

I sat a safe distance from North Linden Jan. I could see her chomping at the bit. She always has something to say.

The eight aldermen sat at the raised crescent shaped table in the meeting room. One member short of the Supreme Court but they felt themselves just as important. Mayor Alonzo Puccinni spoke first, "I'd like to call the meeting to order. Can I have a motion to approve the minutes from the last meeting?"

Two aldermen spoke up, followed by a vote to approve the minutes and enter them into the formal record. This was standard procedure. I had read the minutes and found nothing wrong with them. The mayor continued, "We'll hear from Alderman Sabatini of the first ward."

Our ward, which is his ward, Ward 1, is most impacted by the flooding problem. The DuPage County Forest Preserve District along with the city of Woodland View and FEMA allocated $10 million of government money for flood control. Deciding how to spend it is the subject of tonight's meeting. Alderman Sabatini is the chairman of the Flood Control Committee.

Alderman Sabatini, Angelo, had lived in Woodland View almost as long as I had. Gino and I bought a house here right after Angelo. After Gino died, I sold the house and moved in with Valerie. Angelo, too, came over with the Italian American migration of the late 1960s. Not from Italy, you have to understand. It started in Chicago, mostly Taylor Street more commonly known as Little Italy, with stops in Elmwood Park and Melrose Park. Then eventually continuing the Cadillac wagon train west to Woodland View and nearby Henderson, the furthest West that most of the Italian American pioneers settled in the new territory.

I knew his family. We went way back. Past Little Italy to big Italy. Our grandparents came from a small village on the island of Sicily. There was bad blood across the sea and that bad blood continued in Little Italy. My maiden name was Vinnucci. That's a story for another day.

Alderman Sabatini spoke, "As Chairman of the Flood Control Committee, I've been working with the county and the state reviewing job bids for the flood control project. This involves building a retention pond in the forest behind Linden Avenue. I hope everyone has reviewed the recent report from Chicago Premium Construction. They were responsible for installing the new sewer system. I would like to recommend we accept their bid to build the retention pond. Not only did they submit the lowest bid but they also have prior experience completing projects for Woodland View. We've obtained permission from the Forest Preserve District to build the retention pond which will contain the floodwater. You will find the environmental impact study in your board reports along with all the proper permits from the county."

The second Alderman Sabatini stopped talking, North Linden Jan stood up. She raised her hand but didn't wait to be acknowledged. She said in a brittle voice, "Linden Avenue was torn up for an entire year. There was no parking. My car was constantly dusty. Now we have a brand new street, and we still have flooding. What makes you think Chicago Premium Construction can solve this problem when they couldn't the first time?"

The Mayor pounded his gavel. "Mrs. Culver, the floor is not open for public comments currently. There will be time for public. . ."

"Mr. Mayor, if I may address Mrs. Culver's questions?" Alderman Sabatini asked. He didn't wait for the mayor to answer but turned to North Linden Jan and said, "The Linden Avenue project two years ago was to replace the deteriorated sewer system. It had nothing to do with rainwater control, only the sewer system."

"Why couldn't we fix both at the same time?" North Linden Jan asked.

"It wouldn't have solved the problem. The floodwater system is separate from the sewer system. In reviewing the bids, we believe it is important that the contractor understands both systems," Alderman Sabatini said. "The sewer system and rainwater system have to run on completely different pipes. If you look along Linden Avenue, there are curb drains. Rain water runs into a twelve-inch pipe which then goes back out into the forest preserve and comes up a thirty-inch opening which allows the water to be dispersed over the three hundred acres of forest. That's why we're recommending we hire Chicago Premium Construction because they know the drainage system for Woodland View and they have experience with flood control," Alderman Sabatini said.

"Can you explain in English: why are we still flooding?" North Linden Jan asked.

Good question, I acknowledged.

"We've learned from the engineering surveys that the water currently cannot be dispersed fast enough through the drain. That's why they're recommending we build a retention pond to make it possible to expel the floodwater drains through a larger opening. The $10 million federal grant will fund the project," Alderman Sabatini said.

North Linden Jan didn't get the answers that she wanted. None of us ever do. There are never any answers only lingering questions after city council meetings. After some additional discussion, the council voted unanimously in favor of Alderman Sabatini and Chicago Premium Construction.

The council moved on to other business items. "Next on our agenda is the proposal to increase the budget for animal control. With the upcoming construction in the woods, we expect to see more raccoons in public areas. Streets and Sanitation will be distributing a flyer with recommendations on how to secure residential garbage cans to keep the raccoons out," the mayor said. "We plan to hire an outside contractor, Blue Chip Varmint Control."

"I hear you," a rough looking man in his late fifties with a scraggly gray beard and thick glasses wearing overalls stepped up to the podium and spoke into the microphone. "My name is Jim Reeney. I own Blue Chip Varmint Control. I've done an assessment of the raccoon problem. Well, there seems to be a problem."

My Lord, this guy is going to be trouble, I thought. I could have told him there was a problem, and I didn't need to run any assessment.

"We've already set some baited traps farther back in the woods to capture and release the raccoons at a designated release location. You might see more raccoons on the street and around your house. They tend to learn to avoid the traps." Jim Reeney put this thumbs through his overall suspenders, snapping them as he spoke. He leaned back and forth on his heels.

My Lord, the raccoons are already smarter than this guy, I thought.

"We also will be hunting down the raccoons with tranquilizer guns on designated days. The police will supervise. ."

I couldn't listen anymore. I stood up. "Excuse me, Mr. Mayor, Aldermen, you're going to let this guy walk around our street with a tranquilizer gun? I'd rather take my chances with the raccoons."

"Please, Mrs. Kustodia, sit down," the mayor said. I sat down as North Linden Jan stood up.

"So, what I'm understanding here is that this man will be shooting raccoons in our backyards with tranquilizer guns," North Linden Jan said. "I've got two dogs. Does he know the difference between a terrier and a raccoon? Late at night, can he tell the difference between my Sherlock and Holmes and a raccoon?"

"I hear you," Jim Reeney said. "We won't be entering any backyards, just the woods. If we find any raccoons on public property like the street or the easement, then we will take care of them. We won't be on any private property." He took his baseball cap off and scratched his greasy balding head. It didn't breath confidence in me or the rest of the room. "I assure you we know how these raccoons think. I think like a raccoon."

I thought to myself, that sounds about right. That's the first thing he said that made any sense. The council voted unanimously to hire Blue Chip Varmint Control.

After the meeting adjourned, I stopped Alderman Sabatini in the hallway. "Angelo, can I have a minute?" I asked.

He looked almost relieved to speak with me as North Linden Jan was still talking. She never knows when to keep quiet. Between the raccoons and the retention pond, there was a lot for her to talk about. I almost felt sorry for the alderman. "Mrs. Kustodia, of course. Let's step outside. It's noisy here," he said, darting his eyes back at North Linden Jan.

We stood in the parking lot of city hall. "I spoke with one of the engineers from Chicago Premium Construction when they were out doing the flood survey," I told him. "A very nice young man, Chris Benetti. I recognized the name. It turns out his aunt knew my aunt back from Taylor Street days. Isn't that something?"

"I run into people from the old neighborhood all the time," he said, glancing at his Rolex watch like his time was more precious than mine. He rubbed his chin and then continued, "He's a nice kid. I've spoken with him." He scratched his upper lip. All the tells indicating he was hiding the lies coming out of his mouth. "If there's nothing else, I have to go. Dinner's waiting for me."

I watched him walk away and then hurried to my car to avoid North Linden Jan. I'm sure she was waiting to talk my ear off about something.

## Chapter Nine

The next morning, I went to the Woodland View Public Library. The library is a single one-story building tucked off the road and into the woods. It's dark wood exterior and low windows are reminiscent of prairie design. Prairie design, I learned about that at the book club outing to the Frank Lloyd Wright Home and Studio. Maybe I should start reading some of the book club books. I came to the library not to read, but to talk to my friend, Marian. She usually fills me in on the books for book club so I don't have to read them.

I walked in, stopping by the circulation desk. Marian was sitting behind the wood counter. As head librarian, she doesn't usually work upfront but she was filling in for someone on vacation. Her husband, Nick, and my Gino became best friends in grade school. They introduced us, and we've been friends ever since. Our friendship continued even after Nick and Gino died ten years ago within a few months of each other. Marian kept her job for the benefits.

"Jan, I really enjoyed book club. James has a flair, doesn't he?" Marian said.

I thought to myself. Marian has a thing for James but my

suspicion was she was barking up the wrong tree. James was out of her league. "James does know his way around the kitchen," I said. "Are you going to be at Bingo on Friday?"

"I can't make it. I have to fill in here. We're short staffed," Marian said as she checked out a stack of books for a young child. "I'm going to church on Sunday. Do you want me to pick you up?"

"That would work," I told her, thumbing through the Woodland View community guide. "I was hoping you could help me with some research on the computer."

Marian sighed and said, "Jan, I've offered to help you shop for a computer. You should have one at home. It's not hard to learn. We have classes here."

"No, I don't care for it," I said.

"Ok, let me get someone to watch the front desk. We can go to the computer room." Marian found a clerk to take her spot. We went into a small room previously used for meetings and now transformed into a computer room. There were three computer stations available. Marian sat in front of the computer and clicked on some keys. The computer sprang to life. "Jan, this is the browser we use. It's called Safari. You type your question in the search bar and hit enter. It's pretty simple. What are you looking for?"

"I wanted to look up Chicago Premium Construction." I peered over her shoulder.

Marian typed in the name of the company. A slick website came up. "That's what I wanted." I read the screen. The company was located on the northwest side of Chicago, near Harlem Avenue. "Can we look up who the owner is?" I asked.

Marian clicked a few tabs and different pages popped up. She read them quickly. "It doesn't say on their website but we can look at their incorporation papers," Marian said.

"How do you do that?"

"There's a government website. It's public information." She typed a few words in what she had called the search bar. A long list came back. "Jan, it says here they were incorporated in 1956 in Chicago. The president's name is Michael Stevens, the treasurer was Brad Mitchell. They had twenty employees when they incorporated."

"That doesn't tell me much."

"Jan, what are you looking for?" Marian turned around to look at me.

"I'm looking for the name Benetti."

"It says here that Stevens is also a partner with an Alko Limited."

"Can you look that up?"

Marian typed it in and a long list of files or links as Marian called them came up. "It says they're listed under livery service. They were incorporated the same year, 1956. Their president is listed as Joseph Benetti."

"Interesting," I said, sitting back in the chair away from the glare of the computer. "That's what I was looking for. Thanks, Marian."

Marian turned to me again and asked, "Are you sure you're okay, Jan? I know you put on a brave face at book club."

She was sweet to be concerned about me. "No, really, Marian, I'm fine." I paused and thought for a moment. "Marian, we've been talking about doing a talent show for the National Night Out this year. I know in the past the library has helped by supplying movies. We're not going to do movies this year. Maybe you can help James with the show. We're going to hold auditions over the next few weeks."

Marian's eyes lit up when I mentioned James. "Did James ask me to help?"

"Not specifically. I know he would be very happy to have your help," I said.

"I would love to help anyway I can. The library has a complete collection of karaoke CDs that we rent out. I still have Nick's karaoke machine. Could they use that?" she asked.

"That would make things a lot easier. We'll have to get together with James and figure everything out."

"I want to show you one more thing on the computer before you go." Marian switched the computer back on. "I'm sure you're familiar with Facebook, right?"

"Yeah, Meg and Valerie I know they're all on Facebook. They use it to talk to their friends. It's like a chat room or something."

"It's sort of like that. You can post comments, pictures, videos. You can look for friends online."

"Could you look up Chris Benetti on Facebook?" I asked.

Marian typed in Chris Benetti into what she called the search bar, and a page appeared with pictures of the man I saw last summer. He was wearing swim trunks with a big gold chain, smoking a cigar on a boat.

"That's quite a nice boat for a surveyor," I said.

Marian scrolled down. "These are called friends."

"I know what friends are."

"On Facebook, it means they follow you," Marian said. She clicked on a few faces. I recognized some of the last names. "Jan, I'd like to set up a Facebook page for you. That way when I finally talk you into getting a home computer, you and I can chat."

"Marian, we chat all the time. We're right down the street from each other." I paused. "I like to see people's faces when I'm chatting with them."

"We'll work on that. We'll get you into some computer classes first and talk about it."

"Thanks for your help, Marian," I said, standing up.

# Chapter Ten

I sat on Valerie's front porch in the teak rocking chair that my son-in-law Bill had made for me. He was quite the weekend carpenter, the house was full of his projects. It was nice to watch him teach Danny how to build everything from birdhouses to tree houses.

It was almost ten o'clock and everyone else was getting ready for bed. Around me, I could see lights in the neighboring windows turning off. The Andersons' 65-inch-TV that hung in their living room was casting a shadowy glow through their picture window. I joked with them that if they played a movie I like, I would sit on the bench in front of their house and watch. That image made me think of the old drive-in movie theaters. They laughed and offered to bring me popcorn.

As the lights grew dim, the street grew dark. I couldn't see much. That's why I complain to the mayor about the lack of streetlights. Nobody else seems to mind but the bad guys hide in the dark. The little sneak thieves that they are. And, that's what was bothering me. It wasn't just the meeting or Alderman Sabatini. It was something much deeper than that. It had been bothering me all night. I had to find out what Mr. Hiro was hiding in his shed.

From my vantage point, I could see his house at the end of the block. It is across the street and seven houses down. I would be able to see the white of his panel truck if it was in his driveway but it wasn't. I went up to my apartment and donned the tool belt that my neighbors gave me at Christmas. I put on the windbreaker that said, "Captain, Neighborhood Watch." It was a gift at the annual Andersons' Christmas party. They meant it to be funny in a good-hearted way but I took the responsibility seriously. I grabbed the essentials, my binoculars and a fresh thermos full of Jewel Eight O'Clock Extra Bold coffee and my small notebook and the fountain pen. It was Gino's fountain pen. It was a very special pen considering the person who gave it to him. That's a story for another day. I went back to my rocking chair.

As I sat rocking, it was starting to get cold. I put my hands in the pocket of my windbreaker. I rolled Gino's pen between my fingers. I thought about the adventures Gino and I shared. He was head maître d' at the Sabre Room working his way through medical school at the University of Chicago. Being the head maître d' back in the day gave you a lot of clout. All the stars that came to the shows went through Gino, whether they wanted a special table, special bottle of wine or a special favor. One star that asked Gino for a special favor was Bob Conrad. This was back when he was doing that TV show, *Wild, Wild West*. He was a handsome man, but could get ugly when he drank. He became fast friends with Gino and invited us out to his home in Bear Valley in California. He gave us airplane tickets to Palm Springs and met us there. I was never one for flying but Gino insisted. Then Bob took us up in his small airplane. Bob was an accomplished pilot. In fact, he started the High Sierra Search and Rescue. He said he was going to fly us the rest of the way in his plane. It was the best way to get to his home. He was drunk, and I was terrified. He stopped the plane three or four times along the way at different bars where he drank more. The last stop was at a furniture store because he wanted to look at a couch for his house. I thought I was going insane. We finally landed at the small airstrip behind his lodge. I did the sign of the cross, kissed my rosary and thanked the Virgin Mary. It was a beautiful home resembling a big log cabin. The next morning when we woke up, we found a note from Bob saying he went back to Hollywood to the TV set. Gino and I walked around his kitchen. There was nothing to eat. We walked down the mountainside all the way to the little town and a corner coffee shop. That was an interesting time. We sat and drank coffee all day and laughed about it. It actually turned out to be a really good day. The smell of my Jewel Eight O'Clock Extra Bold reminded me of that morning.

12:30 am. Still no white panel van. I'm glad I grabbed the windbreaker. It was a lovely May night but the woods cool off the street quickly after dark. I could hear the little sneak thieves crawling around the garbage cans on the side of the house. The raccoons weren't my mission tonight. I don't know what time I fell asleep but when I woke up it was 2:30 am. I looked through my binoculars. Mr. Hiro's white van was parked on the slab in his driveway.

The house was dark. I got up and walked down the street. It really was pitch dark at night. There was just enough moonlight to make my way across the street to the front of Mr. Hiro's house. There was not a single light on inside or outside the house. Thankfully like most of the original gas post lights on the block, his didn't work either.

I stepped carefully and quietly through the evergreens and around to the back of the house. The only sound I heard was the gentle waterfall of the koi pond and the crickets singing in the woods. To get to the shed, I stepped onto the koi bridge. The bridge is only two feet wide without railings. I'm still in pretty good shape for seventy-five years old. I do have to admit that my eyesight has gotten a little worse for the wear. One foot in front of the other I took my time, holding my arms out for balance. From the dark water, I could feel the koi watching me, I hoped they would keep my secret.

I reached the shed and looked back at the house again. It was still dark. I tested several cedar planks around the door. They were still nailed tight. I wouldn't be able to move those. I went around to the back. Two of the planks were loose. I pulled on one which popped off, giving me a six-inch window. I grabbed the flashlight from my tool belt and shined it into the darkness. The light hit a pair of eyes that glowed red. I screamed. The little sneak thief jumped out of the shed, knocking me over, carrying something in its mouth. The raccoon took off for the back woods. The porch lights came on and then flood lights lit up the entire back yard. I could see Mr. Hiro running out the back door, grabbing the rake as he ran toward the noise. Towards me.

I took off into the woods as fast as I could. When I felt I was at a safe distance, I hid behind an evergreen, a hundred yards from the light of Mr. Hiro's backyard. I could hear him yelling first in English and then in Japanese. Then I heard Mrs. Hiro answering him back in Japanese.

I stood frozen for what seemed like hours. My feet felt damp and cold in my Keds. The forest smelled moldy. I felt like it was closing in on me. Even after all the lights were off, I stayed hidden. I checked my watch. It was almost 4 a.m. I'd never been in this part of the woods before. There was never a need to. All the years I've been on Linden Avenue, I admired their beauty, and their changes over the seasons. The deep red of the black maples, the orange of the oaks in the fall; the crisp white icicles clinging to the branches in the winter; the cheerful yellow of the daffodils in spring; and the violets and meadow flowers in the summer. The woods are a painting come alive. I even liked the deer as long as they kept their distance.

I heard someone yelling, deep in the woods. My heart pounded. Then I heard it again. I wanted to run away but it sounded like someone needed help. Pulling my flashlight out of my windbreaker, I ran towards the voice. I shined my light on the metal cage that captured Jim Reeney. He was much larger than a raccoon but not much brighter. He stared at me with puppy dog eyes. "I crawled into the cage to change the bait and the door slammed," he said.

I couldn't figure out how even a man as small as Mr. Reeney, physically and mentally, could fit in a cage that size. Apparently he made it work.

"Can you give me a hand here? The latch is broken," he said. "I can't reach my hand through the bars."

I took pliers from my tool belt and pried open the latch, releasing the varmint hunter. He stretched his back. I could hear it crack. "How long have you been in there?" I asked.

"About seven hours," he said after looking at his watch.

"Are you okay?"

"The little beggars took off with the bait."

"If you're fine, I'm going to get going," I said.

"Yeah, I hear you. Thanks a lot." He took his cap off, scratched his head like he was thinking about what to do next and then ran off into the darkness. I stared after him, shaking my head.

I made my way back to my house. The moon was hanging low, and the sun was starting to rise over the horizon. My son-in-law was exiting the front door. He must be on his way to work. He stopped and watched me appear like a ghost as I climbed over the split rail fence out of the forest preserve onto Linden Avenue. I must have looked quite the apparition. My yellow tool belt, my black neighborhood watch windbreaker, my muddy Keds shoes. I was covered in leaves.

I stopped to say good morning but Bill stared at me without saying anything. Smiling and shaking his head, he got in his SUV. I watched him drive down the block and onto Spring Oaks.

I climbed the fifteen long steps to my cozy warm apartment. I walked past the shower and headed to my small bedroom. I was exhausted. I needed rest. I fell onto my Serta Perfect Sleeper and I was out. In an hour my day would start over.

The Postman is Late

## Chapter Eleven

With all the recent excitement, I forgot that I promised James I would attend his friend's art exhibit. It was in the Bucktown area of Chicago. Less than twenty miles from Woodland View, Bucktown couldn't be more different. Once home to Chicago's immigrant population, it has now become a haven for artists and those who fancy themselves artists. Now they call them hipsters. In my day, we called them hippies.

I crammed myself into James' little British car. He told me it was a classic, an MG racing green Midget. It didn't matter to me. I still felt my knees hitting my chin. To match the car, he was wearing his "beret" and leather racing gloves. I made him take the ascot off. James always liked to dress for the occasion. Overdress, in my opinion.

He put the top down. I wrapped my scarf around my hair. I was going to look a mess. We drove down North Avenue, the Chicago skyline lurking in the distance. It was early evening.

"I think you're going to like Angela," James said. "I met her when I was teaching a class on American popular nonfiction. I assigned my students the book the *Devil in the White City.*"

I remembered the title. I wondered if I was supposed to read it for book club but I didn't want to bring it up. James glanced over at me and knew that I had no clue what book he was talking about.

"Jan, you didn't read it, did you?" he asked. "I think you would have found it fascinating. It's set in Chicago during the 1893 World's Fair. It intertwines the story of Daniel H. Burnham, the architect for the fair, with the story of Dr. H.H. Holmes. He was the first known serial killer. He was a real monster. He would lure victims to his hotel and then kill them."

I didn't remember any of this story. I couldn't even picture the book.

"Angela paints portraits of serial killers. I invited her to talk to my class and show some of her paintings. They're very raw and disturbing," James said. "After I met her, I was so intrigued by her point of view that I decided to focus my classes on the depiction of murder in literature."

We arrived in Bucktown. The streets were crowded and parking was limited. The area is a mixture of vintage clothing shops, music clubs, street cafes and warehouses transformed into apartments. What they call vintage, I probably still have hanging in my closet. James drove up and down the street, looking for a parking space. I didn't understand why people wanted to live in this part of Chicago. It was always packed and there was never parking. The restaurants were overpriced, a cup of coffee could set you back seven dollars. That's what I paid for a pound of my Jewel coffee. James comes down here a lot, always raving about this new restaurant or a one-of-a-kind craft store. James considers himself a patron of the arts, any art.

He finally wedged the MG into a space on the street between two large SUVs. They call people who live in Illinois flatlanders because Illinois is as flat as an ironing board. Why people have to drive these large fifty thousand dollar sport utility vehicles is beyond me. There are no mountains to climb.

We got out of the car. I helped James put up the top. We strolled down the street and stopped in front of Gallerie B. People were gathered in front of the Chicago brick repurposed warehouse. James nodded and waved to several of them. I felt out of place in my white capris, pink t-shirt and Keds. They were all wearing black, black jeans, black dresses, black t-shirts. You would think people who enjoyed art would be a little more colorful.

We followed the crowd inside. The interior of the warehouse had been renovated with its brick walls exposed and restored embossed tin ceiling. The floor was roughed up oak. I recognized it as being similar to the floor that was in our first apartment on Taylor Street. Hanging by mere silver threads on the walls were paintings. The first painting I came across was John Wayne Gacy dressed as a clown. His face was covered with spiderwebs. James was right it was very disturbing and raw. I couldn't look away. There was something in his eyes that drew me into the painting. It made me nervous and angry. The next painting was Ted Bundy but he was dressed like a handsome angel. I wasn't sure what Angela was trying to say. These were bad men that did bad things. I definitely wouldn't have any of this in my house.

A waiter wearing a black shirt with a black bowtie offered me a drink. I grabbed the glass, drank it down quickly, grabbed his shoulder and grabbed another one. It was some kind of wine. James walked over with a woman around his age. Maybe a young sixty. Her gray white hair was tied in a long ponytail. She was wearing all black except for a white fuzzy vest. Some kind of faux fur. In this group, I couldn't see anyone wearing real fur.

She was very attractive. I wondered if that's why James was interested in her. They were holding hands and exchanging kisses on the cheek. I thought it would be nice to see James with a girlfriend.

"Jan, I'd like you to meet Angela. She's the genius behind these paintings," James said, leading her over to me.

"Thank you for coming," Angela said, reaching out a hand to shake mine.

She had a strong grip. I liked that.

"What do you think?" She turned her attention to the John Wayne Gacy painting.

To be polite, I gave it another look and shared my own experience. "My friend, Sophie, her husband's first day on the Des Plaines police department was the day they arrested Gacy. He used to bring home the files for her to read. She would read them to me. Not a big fan of Gacy," I said.

"That's so fascinating. I'd love to talk to her or read those files for research for my book," Angela said.

James interrupted. "Angela and her partner are writing a graphic novel about some of the world's most notorious serial killers."

"Our working title is Notorious. I'll have to introduce you to my partner, Karen," Angela said, gazing around the room. She couldn't find who she was seeking and wandered off to talk to someone else.

James took me around the exhibit. We looked at all the paintings. James staring much longer than I did. Angela's work was nice but it wasn't to my taste. I prefer landscapes or flowers or even pet portraits. I sat on one of the wood benches in the center of the room. I was enjoying watching the people more than the paintings. They seemed very full of themselves, each trying to top the other, talking about point of view, depth and brushstrokes. They seemed to be in a competition to win the prize for the most interesting person in the room. My money was on the young guy wearing the black turtleneck and large black-framed glasses and tight black jeans. He seemed to have a personal story about every painting like it was painted for him. People listened and nodded. I took out my handkerchief and giggled into it.

James was in his element, however. He loved to talk. He enjoyed debating and could hold his own with anybody about any subject. I was hoping he'd win the prize tonight. The young man in the black turtleneck watched James and was getting angry. Angela came over and sat next to me. "Aren't you having a good time, Jan?"

"No, Angela, I'm having a very nice time," I said. "You're very talented. It's just that I don't know a lot about fine art."

"You don't need to know a lot about art. It's really about how it makes you feel when you look at a painting," Angela said, standing.

"Come with me."

I followed her and we stood in front of a large painting that took up half the wall. It depicted Richard Speck wearing a nurse's uniform. "How do you feel?" she asked.

I thought about the nurses who I had worked with over the years including the ones who gave their lives to save lives. "Makes me angry," I said.

"All you need to know about art is how it makes you feel," Angela said.

James was right I did like Angela. She was strong and caring. She would make a good wife for him.

The show closed at 11 p.m. I was starving. The little hors d'oeuvres were not to my taste. They were too fancy and too spicy. James offered to walk Angela and Karen home. I recognized Karen immediately as the woman arguing passionately with the man in the turtleneck. Her hair was chestnut brown and cropped short. She wore black army boots, black jeans and a black leather jacket.

"James, do you want to get a bite to eat before we head back?" I asked.

"Our apartment's only a few blocks away. Why don't you come up? I wanted to hear more about the John Wayne Gacy files," Angela said.

"Yes, Angela told me," Karen interjected. "I'd love to hear more. We can make something."

I thought it was nice they could work together and share an apartment. They have to be very good friends to spend that much time together. It must be very convenient. James took Angela's arm in his as we walked. I thought they made a handsome couple. I hoped Karen didn't feel left out. I hoped she had a boyfriend of her own.

We arrived at their Bucktown loft. It was very neat and tidy but small. I figured most of the apartments here were expensive and not large. It was only one bedroom, the couch looked like a pullout. I felt bad for whoever had to sleep on the couch. It didn't look very comfortable. The walls were exposed brick like the art gallery and more of Angela's work hung on it. Apparently people in Bucktown don't like drywall. I don't care much for the unfinished look. It is too untidy.

Karen cracked open the large floor to ceiling glass window to let in fresh air. I could hear the sounds of the city, the horns, people talking. I sat on one of the uncomfortable little wooden chairs. Karen sat across from me on the couch. James and Angela fixed a snack in the kitchen. I could hear them talking about the show. "So, Jan, James told me about the murder on your block," Karen said. "He said you found the body. Do the police know what happened?"

"No, it's still under investigation," I said.

"I'd love to find out more about the investigation. I read a lot of police procedurals," Karen said, sipping on her wine. "And I've interviewed a lot of police officers for the graphic novel Angela and I are working on."

"That's interesting. Karen, what do you do for a living?" I asked.

"I'm a writer. I write for the *Advocate*."

I thought to myself I've never heard of the paper but I didn't want to hurt her feelings so I just nodded.

"Angela and I have been working on this book for years now. I can show you what we've done." Karen ran over to the bookcase and brought out several sketchbooks. "Here are some of the sketches that Angela's done. It started as an episode book and turned into a graphic novel."

Graphic novel, I glanced at the pictures. Fancy way for saying comic book. At least that's what it looked like to me.

"The story is based on real life serial killers. Our characters are a composite of several killers from Jack the Ripper to Aileen Wuomos."

I didn't recognize the name. Karen must have realized it because she continued, "She's the serial killer from Florida whose story is told in *Monster*. You know, the movie?"

No, I didn't know. The last movie I saw with *Monster* in the title was *Monster U*. I watched it with Danny in the tree house.

"Angela and I drove to all the cities where the killings occurred and visited the crime scenes. We looked up the police reports and photos to get more of an insight into the killer's mind. This is the killer in our first book in the series. Her name is Rachel."

I looked at the drawing. Rachel resembled Angelina Jolie to me. In fact all the women in the book were curvy and beautiful. "Are all your killers female?" I asked.

"No, they're all asexual. The female form is the embodiment of beauty in our culture. We use that beauty to contrast the ugliness that lays hidden inside the serial killer."

Intentional or not. It still looked like Angelina Jolie to me. James and Angela brought over four bowls full of bowtie pasta with pine nuts, broccoli and olive oil. I looked hard to find sausage or prosciutto but I got the feeling Angela and Karen were vegetarians.

"So, Jan, Karen has been telling you about our book," Angela said, sitting on the couch next to Karen.

"Yes, it's a very interesting and an unusual topic. What got you interested in serial killers?" I asked.

Angela became quiet and sipped at her wine. With a concerned look, Karen put her hand on Angela's hand. "My parents and I were on vacation at our summer cabin in Minnesota. It was quite beautiful and very secluded. There were only two or three other cabins on the lake and they were back up in the pines. I was nine. I was playing on the beach. Back then parents never watched over your shoulder. It was a different time. I could see the cabin from the beach. I wasn't more than a hundred yards away. I think my mother kept an eye on me from the porch. I couldn't tell but I could feel her watching me." Angela paused, then continued. Her eyes were wet with tears. "When I heard the gunshot, I thought it was fireworks. It was the end of June and the Fourth of July was coming. When I heard the second gunshot I instinctively knew what it was. The echo ran across the lake. I wanted to run to the cabin but I was scared. There were more gunshots peppered throughout the pines. My mind's eye followed the sound of the gunshots as they circled the lake. I was scared. When the police arrived, it was nearly midnight. I was lying in the sand rolled up in a ball. They told me that everyone on the lake was dead but me. It didn't make any sense. No robbery, no purpose, just random evil. That evil took away everything I knew to be my life. My family, my future. I didn't understand why. The killer was never caught and I kept asking that question. I think I still ask why." She paused, picking up one of the sketches. It showed a cabin on a lake, the sky awash with red fireworks dripping like blood. In the woods, a pair of menacing eyes peered out from the darkness.

As she spoke, I could feel her pain. I know what it feels like to lose a loved one to a violent crime. You have two choices. It's like a light switch. If you flip it down, it means you hide in the darkness for the rest of your life. If you flip it up, you walk with the light. I could see that Angela flipped the switch up.

We finished our pasta and polished off the bottle of pinot Grigio. While James cleaned the dishes, Angela showed me more of her artwork. After hearing her talk, I could appreciate her point of view. I could see the sadness in the paintings. Angela explained them to me as we gazed through her portfolio. We came to a painting of a tree in a swamp. There was a pair of shoes hanging from a Cypress tree draped in Spanish moss. "What's this, Angela?"

"It depicts a series of unsolved murders in Louisiana after Katrina."

"Why is there a pair of shoes hanging from a tree?"

"Several rescue workers were found murdered. All of them were missing their shoes. That's why I painted the shoe on the tree," Angela said. "The killer took the shoes as a souvenir. He was never caught."

Vicki Vass

## Chapter Twelve

I arrived at the county offices in Wheaton, Illinois. They sprawl across four or five buildings and several acres. I picked the largest building, which holds the main government offices. The first floor holds the sheriff's office, the county clerk and property assessor. I parked in the parking garage and crossed over the overhead walkway into the building. I am always surprised when walking in that there are no metal detectors.

Located on the third floor is the DuPage County Coroner's office. I carried the tin of cookies that I had made this morning. I know, Sal, the coroner, enjoys my biscotti with his coffee. Sal and I go way back. After I retired from nursing, I worked part time at Jewel, the local grocery store. Sal was in the meat department working his way through medical school. My husband Gino helped him get into the University of Chicago residency program. Working as a butcher helped Sal with his knife skills. Now instead of carving up porterhouse steak, he is carving up cadavers.

After greeting the receptionist and mentioning Sal's name, I made my way to the back office and the break room where I waited for him. After a short period, he came out wearing blue scrubs and wiping his hands on the side of his pants. I hoped he washed his hands. He gave me a big smile. It was obvious he was glad to see me or at least my biscotti. I handed him the tin. "Jan, you brought biscotti. My favorite." He poured himself a mug of coffee and dipped one of the cookies in the coffee. We sat at the small break room table.

He polished off a second biscotti. "Oh, I missed these. I tried Caputo's and Mariano's bakeries but they're nowhere as good as yours."

"The secret is I use lard instead of butter."

"You shouldn't have told me that," he joked, patting his belly, which I noticed had grown substantially. He laughed at his own joke, a loud roar that resounded through my ears. I restrained myself from mentioning either the laugh or his weight gain.

"Sal, I need your help on something," I said. "Gary, our mailman, was brought here a couple days ago."

Eating his third biscotti, Sal looked something up on his iPad. "Here it is, Gary Ingall. Yeah, I did the autopsy myself. I filed the report with the police and the FBI. Some newbie agent came down personally and picked up the report."

"Agent Peabody, I've met him." I nodded.

"Yes, Agent Peabody, Sherman Peabody. I remembered his first name. I thought it was funny. Like the cartoon Sherman and Peabody. Nice enough kid," Sal said.

"Sal, you know I was the one who found Gary," I said.

"You don't say?"

"Can you tell me how he was killed?" I asked.

Sal put down his fourth biscotti and slid his chair closer to my side of the table. Looking around the break room, he whispered, "Jan, you know I could get in trouble. It's an ongoing murder investigation, and the feds are involved. I told you after the last report I gave you that was it. I could lose my job. Even worse I could go to jail." He paused. "Jan, you don't want to get involved."

I grabbed the cookie tin and slid it back to my side of the table. "Gary was my postman. He was my neighbor. He's from my block. I'm already involved."

"Look, Jan, I owe you. I will always owe you. Gino was like a father to me. I wouldn't have made it through med school without his help but you're asking me a lot. If anyone ever finds out I gave you Gino's autopsy report, I will lose my job."

I still have nightmares about that report. What they did to him, what they took from me. "Salvatore, I promise you this is the last favor I ask of you."

Sal signed and nudged me closer. He whispered, "He was beaten to death with a blunt object."

"That's horrible, Sal."

"Yes, it is. Unfortunately I've seen worse," Sal said.

I thought to myself so have I. "Any idea what the weapon was?" I asked.

Sal paused while the receptionist came in, took a yogurt out of the fridge and walked back out. He whispered to me again, "We don't know. I couldn't match the wounds with any similar wounds in the database. I found some kind of fibers but Agent Peabody took them to the FBI lab."

"Well, Sal." I put my hand on top of his. "Thank you so much. Say hi to Maria and the kids. Are they all fine?" I stood up, handing him back the tin.

"Everyone's great," he said with a mouthful of his fifth biscotti.

I turned to glance at him on my way out. "You will send me a copy of Gary's report, won't you?" I asked.

Sal nodded, crumbs around his lips.

## Chapter Thirteen

"Here, test the mic," Roger, James' friend, said to Danny as he helped set up the PA system in the gym.

Danny glanced up at me. I nodded permission. He went onto the stage in the Woodland View Park District gym. Over the years, the Woodland View Police Department received awards for its involvement in the National Night Out crime prevention program. Every year more and more families attend the free event. This year was no exception. The gym was already packed. McGruff, the crime fighting dog, handed out stickers to the kids. Out in the parking lot, kids climbed in and out of police vehicles and fire trucks. Other community groups like the library and park district participated with crime prevention displays, information booths, refreshments, and this year, the talent contest inside the gym.

James was very excited that the Night Out Committee approved his talent show event. He spent weeks planning it and holding rehearsals. Roger set up Marian's karaoke machine. Bill built the small stage in the gym. It was looking to be a fun time. Danny was nervous about playing guitar in front of the rest of the kids. I knew he'd be okay. We practiced *Blackbird* by the Beatles over and over.

James walked onto the stage. He was the emcee for the night. He dressed up for the occasion in a tuxedo with pink striped cummerbund and bowtie. "Ladies and gentleman, welcome to the first annual Woodland View Night Out talent show," James said. The mic squealed. Everyone covered their ears. "Sorry, sorry." James stepped back. After fiddling with the controls, Roger gave him a go-ahead nod. He tapped on the mic. "Once again, we're very excited. We have some of the most talented performers in all of DuPage County," he said, with a flourish, bowing and pointing out to the crowd.

Sitting cross-legged on the gym floor, the kids clapped and cheered. Most of the parents sat on the hard wooden risers. "We'd like to thank our sponsors, Chubby's Drive-Through, the Woodland View Dairy Queen, Target and the Dollar Store for donating prizes for tonight's talent show," James continued talking, pointing to a table where the three judges sat. "Our judging panel includes Police Chief Mark Krundel." The crowd clapped. "Park District Superintendent Tim Guido." The crowd clapped again. "And local recording artist from the band Rebel Reign Dan Dillon. " The crowd went wild, and the kids rose to their feet. James motioned for everyone to sit and settle down. He introduced the first act, North Linden Jan's granddaughter, Becca.

She did a karaoke version of Taylor Swift's *Shake it Off*. I knew the song because Danny and Meg played it for me. Becca was adorable, her ponytails danced as she twirled around the stage. North Linden

Jan stood by the side of the stage, cheering her on and dancing along. Her spindly legs flopped about like a grasshopper.

I sat next to Marian. We watched all the kids. They were all very cute. Danny's friend, Matthew, did a magic act. Monika's niece, Madison, did a dance routine to the song from Frozen. "Who's the guy helping James?" Marian bent over next to me and whispered.

"That's Roger."

"Oh."

"He's very nice. I've met him several times. I don't know if he's divorced or widowed but I do know he's single," I said. "James mentioned that him and Roger go out a lot. They spend a lot of time together. He must not have a girlfriend or wife waiting for him at home."

"That's interesting. He's kind of cute, don't you think?" Marian asked, applying a rosy shade of lipstick.

I studied Roger. I'd never thought about him that way. He was always very neatly dressed and polite but not quite my type.

"What does he do for a living?" Marian asked.

"I'm not sure. He's retired. I think he worked in the fashion industry. I've heard James say that Roger used to be in women's clothing."

"That's interesting."

"I'll introduce you when the show is over," I said. I thought Marian is on the prowl again. I'd never thought about another relationship after Gino passed.

It was Danny's turn to take the stage. He looked so small, standing there. James brought a stool up on stage for Danny to sit on. He sat down and stared out, his eyes wide. All the kids grew quiet. Roger turned the gym lights down and put a spotlight on Danny. He blinked and shaded his eyes. I got a lump in my throat. He appeared so nervous. His first note was a squeaker. He stopped. I wasn't sure if he was going to run off the stage in tears. I went over to stand on the side of the stage. Danny glanced at me. I gave him an encouraging nod.

He strummed softly at first and then grew louder as his confidence grew. He actually broke into a little smile. I could see the kids sitting in the front row, smiling back as they stared up at him.

And, then, the gym doors burst open. Danny stopped playing and everyone turned around to see the source of the noise. The silhouette of Jim Reeney stood in the doorway illuminated by the fluorescent lights in the hallway. He was wearing a helmet, overalls and rubber boots. In his hand, he brandished a tranquilizer dart gun. He was out of breath. "Nobody move," he yelled out in between wheezes and coughs. "Nobody move. I don't know where it is. It could have run in here. It's crazy I tell you. Do you hear me? It's crazy." His gaze, wild with excitement, scanned the gym.

We didn't have a clue what he was ranting about until we heard the squeals. Behind him in the hall, the little sneak thief raccoon ran past him. Jim Reeney took off in pursuit. The door slammed shut behind him. Before I could open it, I heard a thud followed by a scream. And then another thud as his body hit the ground. I ran down the hallway, Chief Krundel hot on my heels. We rolled the body over expecting to see a knife or a bullet wound. What we saw was the three-inch tranquilizer dart sticking out of the bottom of his chin. I pulled it out and checked his vitals. The raccoon outsmarted the varmint hunter once again.

As Chief Krundel called for the EMTs on his radio, I walked down the hallway which was only half lit. I could hear the animal gnawing and hissing in the corner. I carefully picked up one of the small garbage cans that lined the hallway and inched my way closer, quietly. The raccoon stood up on its back hind legs and threw up. The vomit was a mixture of fruit rinds, popcorn and frog legs. I threw the can over the sneak thief. He was not happy. I sat on top of it until animal control arrived to pick him up.

After the excitement was over, Danny and I drove home. I made some popcorn and fresh lemonade. We carried it up to the tree house. Bill had made a small set of stairs on the side of the tree to make the climb easier for me. Danny used the knotted rope that hung from the main branch. The tree house wasn't much larger than my guest bathroom, 5 x 6 feet. We brought sleeping bags, a battery powered lantern and two sets of binoculars for bird watching.

Danny and I keep a notebook to log the birds we've seen. It hangs on a clipboard attached to the side of the tree house. This year we've seen finches, cardinals, blue jays and the red-headed woodpecker. We've seen green and red hummingbirds, a barn owl, a crane, a turkey vulture and yes, one bald eagle. At night, we look at the stars. I've taught Danny how to identify the constellations. Of course, the best time to be up here is the Fourth of July when you can see all the fireworks from the surrounding towns.

The full moon hung low over the old growth oak trees that lined the entrance of the forest preserve. The woods from this view appear ancient, as the cooling forest floor rises a mist into the night. The crickets played their castanets, calling us to sleep. Danny gave out a big yawn. "Gran, Gran, how about a story?" he asked.

I told him a story about his great-grandfather, Gino. As a young man, Gino boxed. He sparred with Jake LaMotta and Rocky Marciano. Danny recognized the name Rocky. I explained to him that this was the real Rocky. As I spoke, I could feel him drifting off, his little eyelids opening and closing. Finally he was out to the world. I looked around the little tree house at my sleeping bag. This was not going to be a comfortable night. At least it was a dry night, not too cool, not too warm. I stuck my head out the window to smell the pines. Breaking through them was the yellow glow of car lights. It was coming up the access road from Woodland View Road into the woods. I couldn't imagine who would be back there at this time of night.

Jim Reeney was at Alexian Brothers Medical Center, recovering from his raccoon fiasco so I knew it wasn't him. I grabbed my binoculars. The car stopped a few hundred yards into the woods. It was a pickup truck. Moments later another car pulled up the access road and parked next to the pickup. It was a dark sedan. I couldn't make out the driver but I recognized the shape of the car. I have seen a lot of Cadillac Sevilles. Both vehicles killed their lights as I watched. I tried hard to make out who the drivers were. A few minutes later the pickup turned on its lights again and took off. Inside the Cadillac, I could see the flick of a lighter, giving just enough glow so I could see Alderman Sabatini lighting his cigar.

## Chapter Fourteen

It was a month since I found Gary. The trail grew cold, colder than Gary. Chief Krundel told me there were no suspects. Agent Peabody told me very little and seemed like he had moved onto other tasks. I guess one less lowly, and in Gary's case lazy, civil servant didn't demand a cry out for justice. He was from Linden Avenue so good or bad he was one of our own. That made it personal to me, and I wasn't going to rest until I knew what happened.

It was now early summer, and South Linden Avenue was returning to normal. I did have to spend time training Gary's replacement, Alex. I think he will work out fine. After I brought in the mail, I waited for Valerie to return from the garden center.

When she arrived, I helped her unload the containers of hostas. Valerie wanted to plant them along the side of the house. I had spent the morning pulling out the Russian sage. They drove me crazy. It grew all wild and every bee in town flocked to it. I couldn't take it anymore. Once I pulled the first one out, the rest were doomed. Valerie couldn't stand a bare space so she ran off to the garden center. I promised to help plant whatever she brought home as long as it wasn't Russian sage.

While she was out, I prepared the soil, adding mushroom compost, pulling out weeds and turning it over. After spending a good part of the morning planting the hostas, we took a break on the front porch, enjoying a glass of fresh iced tea. "Ma, thanks for helping me," Valerie said.

"I am glad to see those Russian sage gone," I told her.

"They were never my favorite," Valerie said.

I agreed with her. We sat in silence and sipped our tea.

"Ma, as I was driving home, I got a call from the bank that's handling Gary's house. I contacted them a few weeks ago about listing the house with me but they told me they went with another agency. I don't know why. That agency is located in the south suburbs near Indiana. They don't know the DuPage area like I do."

"I don't know what they're thinking." I agreed with my daughter. In my mind, she is the best agent in DuPage County. "Have you been in the house?" I asked her.

"No, there was no reason to since I didn't get the listing."

"Is there a lockbox there?"

"I haven't checked. When I drove by I noticed the For Sale sign is already up in front of the house. There must be a lockbox," Valerie said, giving me a wary look.

"Do you want to go in?" I asked her. I knew I did.

"I am curious. I've never been inside," she said, putting down her iced tea glass on the wicker table.

"You should go in. That way you can describe it to any potential buyers. They're going to be new neighbors. They should know what's wrong with the house, right?" I prodded her.

My daughter knows me well. She knows I will wear her down until she gives in so she stood up and said, "Let's go." We walked the few houses down to Gary's. The For Sale sign stood awkwardly in the front yard among the weeds. The brown paint on the cedar siding in front was peeling and green ivy was growing up the side. Gary didn't take very good care of his house or his lawn. It didn't have much curb appeal, and it would be a hard sell with the story attached to it. I was anxious to see the inside. I had talked to him on his porch before but he never invited me in. Normally I'm not one for going places I'm not invited but no invitation was needed today.

"Ma, maybe we shouldn't do this," Valerie said as she unlocked the key lockbox to Gary's house. The house key popped into her hand.

"Valerie, you're a real estate agent. You can go in," I assured her, pushing her forward to the front door.

"Ok, Ma, let's not be long." Valerie unlocked the door and stepped back. We were hit with the smell of mildew from years of water damage. The problem with having a ranch in a flood plain means you have a full basement, and the full basement means you get more floodwater. Gary's house smelled like the damage crept upstairs. We stepped into the small entryway, which opened into the living room. There wasn't much furniture, a lazy-boy recliner, couch and large TV. Gary hadn't updated anything from the original 1960s décor.

I didn't know what I expected to find. The police searched the house before it was cleaned out by the bank and didn't find anything. Or at least that's what Chief Krundel told me. Agent Peabody took a look also but him and I don't talk. Valerie and I wandered through the first floor from the living room to the kitchen to the small bedrooms. "Oh, Valerie, look linoleum kitchen floor. Just like our first house in Chicago, same tile, pink and white squares. And, the wallpaper is foil. It's impossible to get off the wall. This whole house will have to be redone." I pointed out features to her.

Valerie half listened with her cell phone in one ear while checking her iPad mini in the other. Part of the tools of the trade. She was always on some electronic device.

I peeked through the kitchen cabinets. They were empty. The house wasn't much more than three small bedrooms, one full bath, a kitchen and a living room. I opened the door to the basement and got a big whiff of the mildew. Valerie went outside to get a better signal. I clicked on the light and walked down the stairs.

Although finished, the basement lacked furniture or rugs. There was no warmth. I did the circle around the staircase back to the furnace room. Nothing unique. Forced air gas furnace, hot water heater, washer and dryer were still there. It was a nice set of Kenmore, white, extra large capacity. I thought about seeing if the bank would sell it to me. I gave it a good lookover. My husband, Gino, knew his way around appliances so I picked up a couple things about checking out washers and dryers. I pulled the washer away from the wall to get a closer look. The basement was dark except for the one single light bulb dangling over my head and a crack of white sticking out of the wall behind the washing machine.

The whole wall was ugly wood paneling. From the water damage, one of the panels had warped enough where I could stick my hand between the two panels. I reached in and pulled out an envelope addressed to the Andersons. I pulled on the paneling. It popped right off the wall, revealing a large hole that went back to the pea gravel crawl space. I took out my flashlight which I always carry. I shined the light in there. I counted nine U.S. postage bags of mail. Stacks of catalogs, junk mail, packages, some opened, some not. All of them moldy and water damaged. Gary, you little sneak thief, I thought. For whatever reason, he was dumping his day's worth of mail here. The spring floods ruined it so it could never be delivered. On top of one of the bags, I saw a shoebox wrapped in brown paper. I picked it up. It was addressed to Koji Hiro and covered with foreign stamps. It was unopened.

"Ma, are you done?" Valerie called from the top of the stairs. "We got to go."

I wrapped my windbreaker around the box. I put the panel back and pushed the washer back in front of it. "I'm coming, Valerie." I called up the stairs. No need to involve her more than she needed to be. I wasn't sure what to do with the information yet.

# Chapter Fifteen

I sat on my perch and watched my next-door neighbor, Anne Hillstrom, a pleasant young woman in her early forties. She was wearing flowered capri pants. I told her several times that the pants might not be her most flattering look but she wore them anyway. She did crop her long blonde hair like I suggested. She looked cute with her bob haircut. She was looking a little larger since her recent trip to Nashville. I tried to talk her into coming to James' hot yoga class. She always found excuses.

She is a sweet girl but, oh, her house drives me crazy. And, don't get me started on the garage or her car. She thought herself a collector. I might call her a hoarder. All my offers to help her were refused. She is a good neighbor; we watch out for each other so I let it go. I even like Sassy, her white Persian. She is tolerable in her own way.

"Sassy," I heard Anne calling.

"Oh, dear, did she get out again?" I asked, walking down the stairs and over to Anne.

The fence between our yards is only chest high, making it convenient to talk over her knockout roses. "Hey, Jan, yes, Sassy is out again," Anne said. "I was moving a couple things in from the garage and she snuck past me. Have you seen her?"

"No, but I will come help you look." I met Anne in the side yard between our two houses.

We walked up and down the street, calling "Sassy," and looking every which way. There was no answer. I didn't expect one. We stopped in front of Mr. Hiro's place. He was working in the front yard, raking some weeds away from his oriental poppies. He stopped. "Looking for the cat again?" he asked. He pointed to the backyard that was adjacent to his.

As we walked along the side of the abandoned house, we saw Mrs. Hiro raking sand by the koi pond. She glanced up at us, I waved to her. She bowed. She was always very polite. I went over to say hello. I felt a hand grab my shoulder from behind. It was Mr. Hiro, pulling me back. "No," he yelled. He pointed to the ground. I didn't understand. "It's disrespectful to step on the sand."

For the first time, I really saw what Mrs. Hiro was doing. She was making intricate patterns in the sand. Anne watched over my shoulders. I turned to her and said, "When my husband and I lived in Japan, we visited Zen gardens like this. The guide explained that raking the sand is a Japanese art form. Each design tells a story. The circles that she is drawing represent the ripples in a pond as a pebble skips across it. It's beautiful, isn't it, Anne?" I didn't wait for her to answer. I stepped back, said, "Sorry," and bowed to Mrs. Hiro. My shoulder ached from where Mr. Hiro grabbed it. He was very strong. He apologized for grabbing my shoulder.

"The cat is in the house." He pointed to the abandoned house.

Anne and I followed the direction of his finger and stared into the large picture window. There Sassy sat staring out the window at us, watching as if we were her favorite television show. Something dangled out of her mouth. She appeared quite pleased with herself. "Sassy, you bad girl," Anne yelled as she run up the steps to the porch of the bungalow. She tried the door but it was locked. When the door didn't open, Anne turned to me. We were both trying to figure out how Sassy got in. "Jan, I don't understand," she said.

Around the back of the house, we found the stairs that led down to the basement. That's where we saw the doggy door that the nice family's standard poodle used. The bank should have locked the doggy door but it was swinging open. Anne knelt down, swung open the flap and yelled for Sassy. "Come on, Sassy. Come on girl."

Anne reached her arm in as far as it could go. She was able to get her head in, trying to unlock the door. She really had gained weight since Nashville. With the tip of her finger, she was able to flip the deadbolt lock and open the door. I followed her inside and flipped the light switch. No such luck, the utility company shut the electricity off. I took out my flashlight and shone it inside. Sassy jumped at us, scaring the living daylights out of me, knocking the flashlight to the floor. It spun around in a circle like a lighthouse illuminating the basement and the piles of U.S. postal mailbags. Bags were piled up to the ceiling, overflowing with undelivered mail. Gary, you little sneak thief, I said to myself.

I looked at Anne and she looked at me. "What is all this?" Anne asked.

Hours later, Chief Krundel stood in the basement with the postal police as they collected all the undelivered mail. I stood next to him, helping supervise. I offered to deliver it all but the postal police declined my offer. "Chief Krundel, how come nobody searched the house after I found Gary?" I asked him.

He pulled me over to the side out of earshot of the postal police. "It was a matter of jurisdiction between the FBI, Woodland View and the postal police. Between you and me, Jan, the postal police told me they were investigating Gary for months. He wasn't arrested because they couldn't find the evidence. When they did find it after we found Gary, they wanted to see if anyone else was involved."

"It's so strange," I said. "Every day I deliver Bob's mail. You know Bob, he's on oxygen, and he lives two doors down from me. He can't make it out to the mailbox. I asked Gary to bring it to his door but you know how lazy Gary is, I mean was. He tried to stuff everything even packages into the mailbox anything to avoid getting out of the truck. Bob never said that anything was missing."

"Gary knew that you were delivering Bob's mail everyday so he made sure he didn't miss Bob's delivery," Chief Krundel said.

"Most of the mail I saw seemed to be junk mail. Looked like Gary was too lazy to deliver it and dumped it at the abandoned house," I said.

Chief Krundel said, "It's a federal offense if it's shipped through the mail whether it's the coupon saver or a diamond ring. Doesn't matter now anyway." The postal police pulled the chief away.

Walking back outside, I went back to the front of the house. "Hello Agent Peabody," I said as the federal agent stepped out of his standard issue sedan. He was wearing a different suit today. When he saw me, he reached around the back of his collar to double check and make sure the price tag wasn't on it.

"Mrs. Kustodia," he said.

"Jan, please call me Jan, Sherman," I said.

He appeared surprised that I knew his first name. "Jan, yes Jan, tell me what happened."

"The postal police are here. I don't know if I can tell you anything."

"Jan, I'm a special agent of the FBI, you can tell me everything," he said.

I thought about it for a moment. Then I told him about Sassy and the mailbags. I did leave out the part about Mr. Hiro's mysterious package that I found in the hidden wall in the dead postman's basement. It was now safely upstairs in the cabinet under my sink. It's not that I didn't trust Agent Peabody. He seemed like a nice boy. It's just where I come from we don't involve the authorities in neighborhood business.

Once the crime scene was under control, I headed back home. Other than the array of official cars, the street was quiet. I nodded at Helen who was walking Jake. It was almost dinnertime. Valerie and Bill planned to go out for dinner. I was on my own but food wasn't on my mind. I couldn't stop thinking about the package. I'm not one for taking things that don't belong to me but I had my doubts about Mr. Hiro. I needed to know what was in the package before I could get a neighbor in trouble with the police.

After I walked upstairs, I took the package out from under the sink. The brown paper was held together with twine. I set it on the table and stared at it. The return address was from a city I recognized, Gotemba. That was a short distance from Mount Fuji where Gino and I lived.

I grabbed a butcher knife and hacked away at the twine. I tore open the brown paper like a little kid on Christmas morning. Inside was an ornately carved bamboo box. On the lid was a carved image of the peace pagoda from Gotemba. It looked valuable and old. I couldn't see any latch or way to open it.

I poured myself a glass of vino as I pondered the box. I went over to my kitchen sink and gazed out the window. Dark clouds gathered overhead, dark clouds also gathered in my head. I couldn't shake the feeling of dread. I saw Anne in her backyard, chasing Sassy. Serves that cat right, let her stay out in the rain and get wet. Cats hate that.

"Anne," I said out loud, putting my wine glass on the sink and running out to the porch. "Anne," I yelled again from the top deck. "Anne, do you have a minute? Can you come see something?"

Anne grabbed the twenty-pound Persian under her arm. I could see Sassy was not pleased. She opened her back screen door and deposited the cat inside. She went through the side yard and came to the back. "Jan," she said huffing, climbing up the stairs.

I was worried about her. I offered to help her move the treadmill from the garage up to the house but she refused. "Jan, what's up?" She asked.

"Anne, are you still doing that antique hunting stuff?" I asked, opening my screen door.

"Yeah? Do you have something you want to sell? Or, are you looking for something?" Anne's face lit up when I mentioned antiques.

"Come here, I want to show you something." Anne followed me into my kitchen. She stopped to admire the triple tier cookie tray I filled earlier for bingo and then continued to the kitchen table. "Jan, where did you get this?" she asked as she picked up the box and admired it. "Do you know what this is?"

"No, I was hoping you could tell me."

"This is an 19th century Himitsu Bako," Anne said. At my confused look, Anne continued, "It's from the Hakone region of Japan. It's a secret box. It usually holds a good luck charm. These boxes are quite tricky as they have secret moving parts designed to keep people out." Anne examined the corners looking for any part she could squeeze or twist. "I've seen several of these. Some were easy to open, others not so much. This one is very elaborate and valuable. There must be something precious inside." She turned the box over. On the bottom were elaborate carvings of graceful koi. "This is interesting. Usually the boxes are carved with geometrical shapes or lanterns. I've never seen one carved with koi. The peace pagoda carving means it has been blessed by Buddhist monks."

I could see Anne's intensity increasing. She was anxious to solve the puzzle and reveal the contents.

"Look, Jan, when I press on this blue and white koi, one of the most treasured colors for koi, it pushes in." Anne demonstrated. "I think the koi are a combination lock." She pressed the other fish, they all pushed in. 'Oh, dear, it is a combination. We have to press them in order."

"I'll make some tea," I said. After I put the tea on to seep, I brought over the tray of cookies. I could see Anne was very pleased. We worked late into the night. I missed bingo but this was a matter of great urgency. As Anne tried different combinations, I wrote them down on my scratch paper. Finally at 2 am. the box clicked open.

"That's it, that's it, Jan," Anne exclaimed. The top of the bamboo box popped up a half inch. Anne slid it out through the grooves. We both stared inside waiting to see the lost treasure. What we found was a bag of fine white powder. Anne looked at me. "Where did you get this box?"

I thought to myself, oh, no. Mr. Hiro's a drug dealer. He's smuggling narcotics into the country and Gary must have found out. I needed to let Anne know. "It was addressed to Koji Hiro at the end of the block."

"How'd you wind up with it?" Anne asked, setting the box down.

"Anne, I don't want to get you involved. Don't worry about that."

"I'm already involved. We have to give this to the police."

"I can't. How do I explain how I have it and how we opened it?" I said.

Anne thought for a moment and then said, "Let me take it to the lab and test it before we get the police involved and get Mr. Hiro in trouble."

"Could you do that for me?" I asked her. I knew Anne worked as a chemist so it would be easy for her to test the powder. We made a little cut in the bag and I gave Anne a sample to take with her. We both were tired so Anne headed home, carrying a paper plate loaded with cookies. I finished the bottle of Vino.

I sat in what I call my thinking chair. It is an old burgundy leather wingback chair. I brought it with me to every home I ever lived in. It was the first piece of furniture Gino and I bought together for our apartment on Taylor Street. From there the chair traveled to the little Georgian in Melrose Park, our first house together, where Valerie was born. Then it finally stopped here in Woodland View, and that's where the chair will be long after I'm not sitting in it anymore. Sometimes I think I can still smell Gino's cigar smoke if I sniff deep enough into the leather. It was old and worn but sturdy just like me.

It's the chair that I held Valerie in when we brought her home from the hospital, and where I read her her first book. It was the chair where I sat as we watched Walter Kronkite tell us our beloved JFK was assassinated. When Neil Armstrong walked on the moon. The U.S. Hockey team won the gold medal. It's where I sat the day my heart broke, where I learned my Gino was murdered.

## Chapter Sixteen

The next evening, I waited on my porch for Anne to get home from her job at Ebbort Labs. I heard her car from a block away. She needed a new muffler but seemed to have other priorities. Her green Mercury Mystique pulled into the driveway, dripping oil onto the street. I couldn't see her head through the pile of junk that filled her car but I didn't want to bring that up today.

She got out of the car and came over to me. "Hey, Jan, how are you?" she asked.

"Good, Good, Anne. What did you find out?"

"Sea salt and ginseng."

"Sea salt and ginseng," I repeated, not understanding.

"High-grade sea salt and ginseng but that's it," Anne repeated.

"What would you use that for?" I asked.

"I believe because it was sent in an expensive box that was blessed by monks, it is meant to be used for holistic healing," Anne said shuffling from foot to foot.

"Mr. Hiro looks so healthy. He's always working in his garden or on his beautiful koi pond," I said.

"Koi pond?" Anne thought out loud. "That's right, I remember it's in the backyard," she said. Anne thought for another moment and then said, "Sea salt is a holistic cure for sick koi. Even a small percentage in the water kills a lot of harmful bacteria and heals their scales. The ginseng improves their immune system. They must be sick if Mr. Hiro imported a blessed salt from Japan."

"Oh, dear," I thought, "What have I done? I've killed his beautiful koi."

"We have to get this to him," Anne said.

"We should go talk to him," I said. I got up from my chair. We walked down the street to Mr. Hiro's. I held the puzzle box and its precious contents. How would I explain the unwrapped box to Mr. Hiro? Anne trudged behind me.

We knocked on the door. Mrs. Hiro answered, wearing her purple silk kimono with her jet black hair tied in a bun. She bowed gracefully, said nothing and ran retrieving Mr. Hiro. She whispered in Japanese to him, bowed and took off. Mr. Hiro was wearing flip-flops and board shorts and a t-shirt with a surfboard on it. He looked at me and then at Anne. "Trouble with the cat again?"

"Mr. Hiro, I am so sorry. I received this package by mistake and I wanted to return it to you." I handed him the unwrapped package.

He took it, raised his eyebrows and said. "It seems you saved me the trouble of unwrapping it."

I was too embarrassed to answer.

"It's a remedy for my sick fish," he said, holding up the bamboo box.

We stood silent on his porch. "Mr. Hiro, I saw the pond but I didn't see the fish. May I see them?" Anne asked.

He nodded. As we walked to the back of the house, he seemed very pleased to show off his work. Around the yard's perimeter, Japanese pagoda and cement lanterns were scattered among the shrubs that Mr. Hiro called Japanese barberry and weigela. Japanese irises and azalea were nestled in between the shrubs. Lush, green moss danced through the stepping stones.

He pointed out the Asiatic lilies that he planted along the dry riverbed lined with river rocks. It ran the length of the lot from the evergreens to the backwoods. Dotted along the edges were yellow tickseed and meadow sage. A small bamboo bridge traversed under the bloodgood Japanese maple. As we followed him on the stone path by the Zen garden, Anne marveled at a stone statue of a graceful and elegant kneeling woman with her hands clasped in prayer. Anne stepped toward her. Mr. Hiro grabbed her and pulled her back before her foot touched the sand. Anne was shocked.

He took his finger and shook it in front of her, motioning, "No." He said, "I'm so sorry but that is very disrespectful. My wife takes great care with her garden."

"I apologize. I wasn't paying attention," Anne said. "I wanted to see the statue. She's fabulous."

"That statue is a Ishi no Koe. It means voice of the stone. It's a way to honor our departed ancestors," Mr. Hiro said.

"For Italians, it's Mother Mary in a bathtub," I said. At Mr. Hiro's confused expression, I explained, "It's a homemade shrine to the virgin using an old claw foot bathtub. You put the bathtub upended in the ground. It makes an arched alcove. The inside of the bathtub is usually painted sky blue with clouds. You place the statue of the virgin Mary in her little house and plant flowers around to complete the shrine."

"I've seen those statues," Mr. Hiro said. "Our tradition is called Satori. It's the Japanese word for enlightenment. We believe the Zen garden should be used for reflection and meditation which brings us to enlightenment. This helps us understand who we are and our place in the world."

"That's a very lovely sentiment. I find enlightenment through appreciating antiques. Holding an antique is like touching history," Anne said, gazing around her surroundings. "Your yard is very beautiful, Mr. Hiro."

"Please Koji," he said interrupting. "Thank you. My wife would be very honored that you say that."

"My friend in St. Charles is very interested in Japanese culture and has traveled there several times to study Zen gardens. She designs and builds authentic gardens for her clients here in the U.S. She would be very impressed by your work. May I take pictures? I'd love to show her this," Anne said.

Now Koji was smiling ear to ear. He nodded his permission. Anne snapped pictures with her phone. She walked onto the bridge as the koi circled and splashed around her like playful children. Koji spoke, "Since the early spring rains, my koi have not been well. You can see some of their scales are falling off. Their tails have tail rot. I've increased the filtration. I've given them more fresh vegetables with lots of Vitamin C to build up their immune systems. The water is clear. I hoped the blessed salt would kill whatever is hurting my fish."

Anne reached down into the water and petted one of the larger koi. "Yes, I see the scale damage, Koji. Have you tested the water?"

"Just for the pH and alkaline levels. Temperature, everything is good."

"Do you mind if I take a sample to my lab?"

"Please, please," he said with a bow.

I handed Anne a little plastic baggie from the stash that I always carried in my pocket. She filled it with pond water. As Koji and Anne talked, I noticed Mrs. Hiro peeking out the kitchen window at us. She saw me notice her and closed the curtains quickly.

"Koji, I could ask my friend from St. Charles to look at your fish. She's wonderful with koi. In fact, people call her the koi whisperer," Anne said. "She has a sanctuary where she heals sick koi."

Koji smiled and bowed again. I thought to myself. This is a man who respects life, not one who would take a life.

Anne and I left Koji's home. We stood in front of his house, I hugged her, and she headed back to her house. I heard shouting coming from the other direction. I ran towards the noise. A rusty tan van with the name Blue Chip Varmint Control handwritten on the side was parked in front of North Linden Jan's house. Her back yard gate flew open, and Jim Reeney came running out followed by a broom-wielding North Linden Jan. She was on his heels swatting him and cursing. Her two little terriers, Sherlock and Holmes, barking and chasing behind her. Jim Reeney ran to his driver's side door. He pulled on it, it was locked. He peered inside. "Damn, I locked my keys inside again."

Dropping the tranquilizer gun, it fired and shot him in the calf. Hopping on one foot, he turned around to face the music as North Linden Jan landed the edge of the O'Cedar sweeper on the side of his face. His jaw quivered from the impact.

"Jan, what are you doing?" I yelled. I pulled her off before she could swat him again. Sherlock and Holmes danced around, nipping at the varmint hunter's ankles. "Jan, what's going on?"

"This idiot was in my backyard," North Linden Jan said.

"I saw a raccoon run into your backyard. I heard your dogs barking. I thought they could be in danger," Jim Reeney said, clutching his leg. A bit of drool dripped from the corner of his mouth. He appeared rabid.

"The only danger was from you." She swatted at him again with the broom. The terriers hopped and barked and nipped.

Jim Reeney's eyes started to close, his legs got wobbly. I grabbed him by the arm. "You better sit down." He slid down the side of the van, landing on the curb.

"It was a really big raccoon. It was the one that trapped me in the cage in the woods. He's had it out for me since day one. He's the leader, you hear me?" He slurred his words and tipped over. He was out.

For the final insult, Sherlock and Holmes lifted their legs and marked Jim Reeney. I turned to Jan and said, "You better call 911."

Vicki Vass

## Chapter Seventeen

It was a perfect summer morning but I could tell it was going to get hot. It was already in the mid 70s. I made my newspaper deliveries and saw a raccoon slinking along Helen's curbside evergreens. They were getting bolder. They usually weren't out at this time of day. The sneak thief stood up on its hind legs and hissed at me. In its claw was a piece of meat. Its mouth was all crusty and bloody. I thought the blood was from whatever it was eating but then it fell over dead.

Jim Reeney was back in Alexian Brothers, recovering from his last tranquilizer dart battle. I wouldn't call him anyway. I went home, got a shovel and a black garbage bag. I shoveled the raccoon into the bag, tied it up tight and threw him in my Saturn's trunk. I drove to the animal clinic, which was adjacent to the dog park. I didn't want to leave the raccoon on the sidewalk. I was worried the kids might touch it on their way to summer camp.

I left the raccoon in the trunk and went inside the Woodland View Animal Clinic. "Hi Audrey," I said to the veterinary assistant. I met her during the annual pet lover's fair the park district holds every fall.

The fair features demonstrations, animal adoption booths and local pet-related crafts. I felt a little hypocritical wearing the t-shirt "I heart PAWs," but I liked helping out at community events. "Is Dr. Grover available? I have an emergency." I asked her.

Audrey went in the back room and retrieved Dr. Grover, a nice young man with shaggy brown hair and puppy dog eyes. "What's the emergency, Jan?"

"Doc, come with me. It's out in my trunk." He followed me out the clinic doors. I opened the trunk, and he opened the bag. He closed the bag up and brought the raccoon into one of his examination rooms. I followed behind him.

"Where'd you find this, Jan?" He set the bag on the steel examination table.

"It was just walking down our street. It hissed at me and dropped dead," I said. "It looks sick like the raccoon from the night out."

"What are you talking about?"

"The night of the National Night Out, a raccoon got in the building. His mouth was all crusty and bloody. He was hissing and shaking like this one. I threw a garbage can over him until the county animal control guys came."

"I'll contact them to see if they did an autopsy," Dr. Grover said. He donned surgical gloves and examined the raccoon's mouth. "This guy ate something pretty bad. He's been throwing up blood. Raccoons have a high tolerance for spoiled food so this is unusual."

"The raccoon at the Night Out threw up frog legs," I said.

"I'll find out what he's been into once I cut him open," Dr.

Grover said, taking the gloves off and washing his hands.

I left the clinic after Dr. Grover promised to call me with the autopsy results. I could see over to the dog park from where I was parked. Helen and Jake the corgi were entering the park. Helen let Jake off his leash. The small dog ran to play with the other dogs.

I saw a young frazzled woman stapling a flyer to the wood signboard by the gate of the dog park. Standing next to her was a young boy holding an empty leash. I walked over to read the sign. It was a picture of a puppy that read, "Missing, Bernese mountain dog."

"Is that your dog?" I asked her.

"Yes." She ran a hand through her unwashed red hair.

"What happened? Did he run away?"

"No, I put him in the backyard while I was making lunch for my son. We heard the gate open. By the time I ran out, he was gone. Somebody opened the gate," she said.

I hoped it wasn't Jim Reeney. "You didn't see an ugly brown van in front of your house?" I asked.

She stopped to think. "The street was empty."

"Do you think somebody stole your puppy?" I asked.

"I don't know." I could see she was holding back her tears. I looked down at the boy.

"What's your name?"

"Tyler," he said.

"What's your puppy's name?"

"Rocky."

Even though I'm not a dog enthusiast, the thought of some sneak thief taking a puppy away from this sweet little boy made my blood boil. "We're going to find Rocky for you."

"You mean it?" he asked.

"It's a promise," I said. I could tell his mother wasn't as trusting as Tyler. "Where do you live?" I asked her.

"We're on North Linden, just a few blocks from here."

"I live on South Linden. We're neighbors. I'm Jan," I said.

"Jennifer," she replied, handing me a flyer.

"What time did this happen?"

"About lunchtime yesterday," Jennifer said. "Tyler's heartbroken. My husband gave him the puppy before he left for his tour in Afghanistan. Tyler was worried about his father so Jim, that's my husband's name, told Tyler to take care of Rocky. When he returned, they would train Rocky together."

"That's so sad," I said. My heart went out to this family. "Did you call the police? Were they able to help you?"

"They came over yesterday. There's nothing they can do. They didn't find anything in the yard," Jennifer said. "They did say there were reports of other dogs taken from yards a few towns over."

I knelt down and gazed at Tyler. "I know a lot of people. I'm going to take care of this for you. Okay?"

The boy nodded solemnly. "Pinky swear?" He held up his pinky.

I locked mine in his and repeated, "Pinky swear."

Taking a flyer from Jennifer so I would have her phone number, I went back to my car. When I got home, I made myself a cup of coffee. I pulled out my small notepad I always carried and my fountain pen. About a year ago, there were a bunch of car break-ins up and down Linden Avenue. I started writing down license plates of cars that I knew didn't belong on the block. There was one car that kept driving down our dead end street, never parking. I waited on my porch and watched him until one day I saw him trying to break into Pete's car. I called the police and then I chased him into the woods. Ever since that day I've carried my notepad and my fountain pen with me. This green Waterman fountain pen is dear to me. It was dear to Gino.

There were only two unknown license plates in my notebook that I wrote down from yesterday. One was a motorcycle, the other a pickup truck with a camper on the back. I checked back on Tuesday and Wednesday. That same pickup truck was driving up and down Linden. At first I thought he was one of the recycling scavengers who cruised down our street on garbage day looking for metal scraps. But not three days in a row.

I called Chief Krundel. "Mark, it's Jan. I need a favor. Can you run a license plate for me?" I asked him.

"Jan, what's going on?" he asked.

"Mark, I don't want to get into details. Please do me this favor." After I got the address, I loaded up my Saturn with supplies. I headed over to North Linden Jan's house. I felt obligated since Jennifer and Tyler were her neighbors. She was outside watering her hostas.

Getting out of my car, I walked up to her and handed her the flyer. "Yeah, Jan, I know. That's Jennifer. She lives a block down. I helped her put these up around the block. When I saw her earlier, she was going to the dog park to see if anyone saw her dog," North Linden Jan said. "I feel terrible about it."

"Do you want to take a ride with me?" I asked.

"Where?" She gave me a suspicious look.

"I've got a lead."

"Have you contacted the police?"

"This is a neighborhood problem. We have to take care of it," I said. "Get in the car." North Linden Avenue Jan got in my trusted Saturn. We drove to Glendale Heights, a neighboring suburb. "Jan, I read an article a few weeks back in the *Daily Herald* about dogfighting rings. They were stealing dogs from backyards to use them as training bait for the fighting dogs. That's why we're not calling the police. We can't let this happen in our neighborhood or any neighborhood," I said. "Besides we have to make sure this is the right guy before we get the police involved."

We arrived at the small ranch clad in green aluminum siding, a six-foot high chain link fence surrounded the entire lot. The house backed up to the highway underpass. It was run down, weeds were growing out of the cracks. There was a large brown pitbull chained to the tree around the back of the house. The poor thing must have been out in the sun all day. He was lying on the hot cement and panting heavily.

I went to my trunk to get our supplies. I grabbed the two Louisville sluggers and threw one over to Jan. She caught it with a surprised look on her face. "What's this for?" she asked.

"Just in case," I told her. Parked in the driveway sat the red pickup truck that I saw driving up and down on our block. Its license plate matched the one I wrote down. The overhead garage door hung by its hinges, it was dented and broken. As we moved towards it, I could hear dogs whining and whimpering from inside the garage.

"Jan, I don't feel right about this. What if this is the wrong house? Or even worse what if it's the right house?" North Linden Jan said.

"Let's take a look," I said. We pulled on the broken garage door trying to raise it but it was stuck. I could hear the whine of a puppy. I peeked through the opening and saw crates and boxes, all of them covered with tarps. Together, Jan and I tried to lift the heavy overhead door. It rattled and groaned. We tried again. This time the whole door fell off towards us. We both jumped back in time to avoid getting crushed. "Hurry, Jan," I yelled. We took the tarps off the cages revealing three dogs all different breeds and sizes. In the fourth cage, I found Rocky, the little Bernese. It had to be at least 90 degrees in the garage. All the dogs were panting heavily.

"What do we do now?" Jan asked.

The garage door leading to the house flung open. A very large man wearing cut-off jean shorts and a rebel flag t-shirt flew out, waving his heavily tattooed arms and yelling. His beer gut popped out from underneath the short t-shirt. His face was bright red from exertion and alcohol. He grabbed my shoulder with his sweaty hand. "Who the hell are you?" he asked.

I gave him the only answer I could think of. I hit him in the knee with the Louisville Slugger. He fell to the garage floor, clutching his knee and crying. Jan followed with a bunt to the forehead. "That's for Sherlock." And then she slammed the bat back down, this one was a home run. "That one's for Holmes." He lay on the floor, moaning and rolling around.

I searched around the shelves and found orange outdoor extension cords. Jan and I wrapped him up tight. Jan ran outside and got the hose. We watered the dogs. Their little tails wagged in appreciation. When we finished watering them, I turned the hose on the sneak thief. I knew something about waterboarding but the police would be here soon so I made the best of the time that was left. I wrote down the list of names he shouted out, his sneak thief companions, who were stealing and fighting these poor creatures, they would be dealt with. I pinned the list to his chest with a staple gun.

Chief Krundel was the first officer to respond, he recognized the address as the one he gave me earlier. "Jan, you got to get out of here. I'll take care of this," he said.

North Linden Avenue Jan and I grabbed the Bernese. "Chief, look after the other dogs. We're going to take this one. We know its owner," I said.

Chief Krundel handcuffed the man who was still on the ground. The last thing I heard him say as we got in the car was, "I have two dogs. One is Bandit and the other's name is Archer." I could hear the thuds and yells as Chief Krundel's nightstick made sure our neighborhood dogs would be safe in the future. I rolled up my window to muffle the screams. I felt comfortable leaving Chief Krundel in charge of the animals. The one chained in the yard and the one handcuffed in the garage.

North Linden Jan was shaking, sitting next to me. She was holding the Bernese puppy who was still whining. We pulled up in front of Jennifer's house.

I grabbed Rocky, holding him gently. I could tell Jan was still shook up. Her silence said it all. She followed me out of the car and to the door. I knocked on the door. Tyler opened it. "Tyler, how many times have I told you. . ." Jennifer came out from the kitchen, yelling at him.

He didn't hear her. He was bent down, hugging the puppy who was wiggling in his arms and whimpering. Tears ran down his cheeks. Jennifer stared in disbelief. Tyler hugged my leg. "Pinky swear," I said.

"Thank you so much," Jennifer said, her eyes glistening. We both hugged her and then North Linden Jan and I each went our separate ways.

## Chapter Eighteen

Most people from Chicago know Taylor Street. It's more than just a street; it's a neighborhood. Located on the near southeast side of Chicago off I-290 bordered by Halsted to the east and Ashland Avenue to the west, Taylor Street is known as Little Italy. It's where I grew up.

My younger sister, Donna, still lives in the two flat that our parents owned. We don't speak much anymore since my husband passed. It's not that we don't get along, it's just we don't have much in common. I left Taylor Street in my rearview mirror and I didn't look back. Donna and her husband, Sammy, couldn't leave Taylor Street. Sammy was in the business. My Gino was different. Gino was a family man, a hard-working family man. He worked in the emergency room at Cook County Hospital. Even as a resident, he kept his nighttime job as head maitre d at the Sabre Room. In its day the Sabre Room was as close to Vegas as Chicago could get. It even had its own showgirls, I was one of them. The Chicago people liked my Gino and trusted him but knew not to get him involved.

Today I needed Donna's help. I was meeting her at Rosebud, one of Chicago's original Italian restaurants. I did miss real Italian food. Once you move west of Western Avenue in Chicago, all the Italian food even at the best restaurants is all precooked or frozen. For authentic Italian you have to go to Taylor Street or cook it yourself.

Leading me to a corner leather clad booth, the host set down a menu and went back to his station. Donna was late. She was always late even when we were kids. I ordered a house made lemonade while I waited. It was tart, just like I remembered. Donna finally arrived. Her long blonde hair fanned around her, sprayed and teased to within an inch of its life. Her tight jeans clung to her thighs; her leopard print blouse was open to her bra and her stilettos clicked on the clay tile floor of the restaurant. All a little inappropriate for her age, I thought, but she thought she could pull it off. Her way of reminding me she is my younger sister even if it's only by a year. "Am I late?" she asked, sitting down. She knew she was but didn't care.

I didn't bother answering. "Did you dye your hair?" I asked.

"No, it's always been blonde." Donna pulled off her designer sunglasses and put them in her purse. Her long nails danced on the table.

Strange, that's not how I remembered her hair. It was naturally darker than mine. "How you been, D? How's Sammy?"

"Good. He's still working. He's always busy. I've been busy, too. I'm in the middle of redoing the kitchen so I've got contractors in and out all day," Donna said. "We got rid of all the old cabinets, the pink and white linoleum is gone. We're putting in granite countertops, slate floor and maple cabinets. Everything I'm taking out of the kitchen, I'm moving to the kitchen in the basement. Oh, and, I booked a cruise for the end of August. Twenty-one days to Italy and the islands. I'm making Sammy take time off," Donna said.

"That's great, D, that's really great."

"So, Jan, it's been three, four years?" Donna thought for a moment and then remembered. "It was the Rossini's wedding. Michael and Rita, right?"

"Yea, D, I think that's the last time we saw each other."

Donna put her hand over my hand. I noticed her nails were perfect and she upgraded her diamond ring again to a three-carat stunner. "Jan, why don't we get together more often?" she asked. "Why is it only every three, four years? What's happened to us?"

"D, you won't leave Chicago. I've invited you out to the house. Valerie's invited you out. We invited you for Christmas, for Danny's birthday party."

"Jan, you know Sammy's always busy. And the traffic heading out of Chicago, forget about it."

I knew this conversation wasn't going anywhere. It's the same one we have every time we get together. You only see the people you really want to see. We ordered lunch. I ordered the ricotta gnocchi with a tomato cream sauce, Donna ordered a tuna nicoise salad without dressing. I nibbled on the fresh baked Italian bread and the parmesan sticks. Donna sipped her water.

I passed on dessert. "D, let's walk over and get an ice, Ok?" I asked. Donna paid for lunch. She insisted. We strolled down Taylor Street and headed east passing by many of the shops. Most of them were new since I had been here last. It seemed like even Taylor Street was being hit by the hipsters or yuppies or whatever they call themselves nowadays with their overpriced little boutiques. "D, what happened to Francis' butcher shop?"

"That old place – it closed years ago. Nobody goes to butcher shops anymore. There's a Whole Foods on the next block." Donna clutched her Versace oversized purse.

"Remember over the butcher shop, Mary, Francis' daughter. She used to pull the blinds up and down to let her boyfriend know it was safe for her to sneak out. Remember? Remember Mary?"

"Yeah, Jan, she's dead. She died like ten years ago."

"Oh," I said. We reached Mario's Italian Ice stand, the best and only real Italian ice in Chicago. Fresh, cold, sweet. I got the combination lemonade and watermelon. Donna passed. "This is so good, D. You can't get any good food in the suburbs. I swear to God. Do you know they tried opening an Al's beef in Henderson?"

"Shut up," she said.

"No, I mean it. I went in and talked to the manager when they opened. He said they bought the name. It's not the same beef. It's not even the same family. Guess what?"

"What?"

"It's not the same sandwich. They closed after a year."

"That's what I'm saying, Jan, everything you need is on this street. This is the neighborhood, this is our neighborhood. Why you wanted to leave, I'll never know."

I couldn't believe that she didn't understand. I couldn't live in a neighborhood with the type of men responsible for my Gino's death. And, she would never understand. She lived that life, Gino and I escaped from it. All right, I put it off long enough, and I asked her what I came to ask her. "D, does Sammy have any business with the Benettis?"

"Jan, you know family doesn't talk business," Donna said, evading my question. Her brown eyes were covered by her oversized sunglasses.

"C'mon, D, I know that you hear things. The Benettis and the Sabatinis have business together, don't they?"

Donna was quiet.

"Angelo Sabatini's an alderman in Woodland View. He's my alderman. He's up to something. I have to find out what it is." I told her, finishing my ice. I tossed the empty container in a nearby garbage can. "Can you ask around? Talk to some of the wives. Casual like. Can you do that for me?"

Donna was still quiet. "Jan, I'll do this thing for you because you're my sister, and I love you. Let's not speak about this again."

She left me standing on the corner. I pulled my keys out of my purse and headed towards Western Avenue where I'd parked the Saturn. This wasn't my neighborhood anymore. It felt unfamiliar. These were the streets that D and I played on as kids. Our mom making Sunday gravy on the second floor while we played jacks in the alley. The corner ice cream shop is gone where I had my first kiss. No, this wasn't my neighborhood anymore.

I felt rather than heard footsteps behind me. The afternoon sun cast shadows along the brick storefronts. I glanced over my shoulder. The Chicago skyline loomed in the distance. Something didn't feel right. Not just that I didn't belong here anymore. It was a feeling I was being followed. Strange, I was surrounded by people, heading about their business. But they didn't bother me. There was someone around me whose business was me.

I'm used to looking over my shoulder, waiting for the past to catch up with me. But this wouldn't be the day so I quickened my pace and reached the corner of Western Avenue and Taylor Street. I turned south. Just another block. I could see the gray Saturn with its sunflower hanging off the antenna. Now my quick walk turned into a run. I reached the door handle and fumbled with my keys, scratching up the paint around the keyhole. I jumped in the Saturn, locked the doors, started the engine and hit the gas. I nearly clipped the Lexus that was parked in front of me. As I glanced in the rearview mirror, I saw people walking up and down Western Avenue, not running, not looking over their shoulders, moving along about their everyday business. I smiled feeling a bit foolish like I had overreacted. And, then I saw a large man in a shiny suit run around the corner, stopping in the middle of the street watching me drive off.

## Chapter Nineteen

I met Anne and her friend in front of Mr. Hiro's house. Drops of rainwater from the night before still clung to his flowers. Last night was another bad storm but the flooding was not as severe as what we experienced earlier in the spring.

Anne's friend was quite interesting. Staring at me, her greenish blue eyes locked into mine, not blinking once. Her long black hair was braided into a ponytail that reached her hips. Her long maxi skirt dusted the tops of the hearty Rozanne purple geraniums that lined Mr. Hiro's walkway. She was dressed like a gypsy. In the 1970s we called them hippies. From the minute we met, I could tell she had an old soul but a young heart. Anne introduced her as "N."

"Nice to meet you, N, how do you spell that?"

"Just N," she said. She shrugged.

"Does that stand for something?" I asked.

"No, just N."

"Anne tells me you do koi rescue. That's very interesting. How do you rescue a koi?"

She hugged me. I backed away. Oh, great, a hugger, I thought.

"Jan, it's more than rescuing the koi. I bring them back to health with holistic medicines combined with love and light. I have a whole sanctuary not just for the koi but where people can come and refresh their souls. My refuge has an outdoor yoga studio and an indoor spa for healing massage." As she spoke, the bracelets on her wrist jingled and her hands swayed in the air like a hypnotic dance. I felt myself drifting away. I could see the kindness that lay beneath her costume exterior. "Every koi is a being. They feel."

"Mr. Hiro's fish are quite sick. We hope you can help with them," I said as we knocked on his door. Mr. Hiro opened it. We introduced him to N, who spoke to him in Japanese. Mr. Hiro was quite pleased to speak to her in his native tongue. They did their greetings and bows. We followed Mr. Hiro and N back to the koi pond.

"Mr. Hiro, this garden is lovely. I feel the light." N swirled around, taking in the garden. "The aura is quite powerful. It reminds of the garden in Kyoto." N walked the bridge and knelt down to touch the koi. With the large red poppies hiding my view of the bridge, she appeared to be walking on water. I moved closer to make sure she wasn't. She spoke in Japanese to the koi and listened carefully as if waiting to hear them reply. She examined their scales. "Mr. Hiro, your fish are quite sick. There's a bacteria in the water. Have you introduced any new fish recently?"

Mr. Hiro shook his head no.

"Something is bringing this bacteria into the water," N said, sitting back on her heels and staring at the pond.

Mr. Hiro carried the Japanese puzzle box with its sea salt and ginseng to the bridge. They sprinkled it over the water and gave a blessing in Japanese. N walked around the edge of the pond, examining the water plants. She appeared to be looking for any signs of what was causing the sickness. Mr. Hiro followed behind her. They stopped at the shed.

Mr. Hiro examined the missing plank I pulled off a few days earlier. He held the loose plank up and stared at me. I glanced down at the ground. N bent down and picked something off the ground. She came back over the bridge and held her hand out. In it was a dead frog. "This frog died from a condition called red leg. It's caused by Aeromonas hydrophila. The frog was exposed to contaminated water. He brought the bacteria into the koi pond. It infected the fish, causing the tail rot and the lesions on the scales," N said.

"Oh, dear, how do we fix this?" I asked.

"You have to raise the saline level in the water. It will kill the bacteria. The blessing salt is a good start. You will need a hundred pounds of solar salt. I also would increase the koi's vitamin C to help them combat the bacteria. They should be fine," N said.

As the koi whisperer and Mr. Hiro reviewed the game plan, I thought for a moment. I recalled the dead frog I found in the woods during our book club picnic and the raccoon at the talent show throwing up frog legs. "I saw a dead frog in the woods the other day," I told them.

"Take me to it. I want to see if it died of the same condition," N said.

I led them through the path and to the boggy spot where I saw the dead frog. N and Anne both held their noses. 'It smells like raw sewage," Anne said.

Before we even reached the spot where I found the bullfrog, we saw at least a dozen dead frogs. Some decayed, others still intact with red sores. The koi whisperer knelt down. She turned to Mr. Hiro. "This is what has been causing all your problems. This water must be contaminated. It's caused the red leg in the frog and they've been entering your pond. You're going to continue having this problem until you find out what is contaminating the frogs."

Staring down at the ground, we walked along the bog until we came to a large sewer. "This is what Alderman Sabatini was talking about at the floodwater meeting," I said. "This is where all the rain water that flows into the curb drains ends up."

"This sure isn't rain water," Anne said, holding her nose.

N took a sample in a small vial. We headed to the mayor's office. His clerk Nancy, who is one of the Bunco regulars, recognized me. She was the first to greet us outside his office. "Nancy, is the mayor in?" I asked.

"Jan, he's in but he's busy," she said. "I can check his schedule if you want to make an appointment."

"I don't have time for that." I brushed past her and opened the door to his office. He was sitting at the government issue wood desk, staring at his computer. Anne and N followed me into his office.

"Mayor, I want to talk to you," I said.

"What do you need, Jan?" The mayor asked.

I placed the vial of water on his desk and N put the baggie with the dead frog next to it. "What is this?" The mayor asked.

"This is contaminated water from the woods behind our street. It's killing frogs," I told him.

"What are you talking about?" the mayor asked, lifting up the vial and staring at it.

"There's raw sewage coming up from the floodwater drain."

"That's impossible. It's two separate systems."

"It might be impossible but it's happening, " I told him, crossing my arms over my chest.

The mayor picked up the phone and contacted the head of streets and sanitation. "Roy's going to check it out."

"I'll meet him back by the drain so he can see for himself," I said, leaving the mayor's office.

I went back to the woods where I waited for Roy. A short while later, he walked up to me, his work boots squishing in the boggy mud. "Wow, Jan, this is pretty bad. I didn't know this was happening," he said, eying the dead frogs.

"When I was out here for a picnic for book club, the ground was dry. The sewage only comes up during a bad rain," I told him.

"We'll look into it," Roy said.

Look into it, government speak for we don't know what we're doing but we will spend a lot of money and we still won't know what we're doing. I reached my limit. "Bye, Roy," I said to him, stepping through the boggy mud out of the forest and through the side yard by James' house.

Reaching the front of his house, I glanced next door and saw

Alderman Sabatini sitting on a lawn chair in his garage with a cigar in one hand and a bottle of Scotch in the other. I'm going to stop this now. I crossed the lawn and stood in front of him. He continued puffing away.

The alderman's garage is what people call man caves nowadays. Italian men like to sit in their garage, watching people walk up and down the street. Gino was the same way. Alderman Sabatini's garage wall was decorated with posters from *Goodfellas*, the Rat Pack at the Sands Hotel and the 1985 Chicago Bears. A pinball machine was next to his Snap-on mechanics' tool cabinet. His usually clean and polished black Cadillac Seville was dusty and caked with mud. This was not the Italian way.

He took a big puff and blew out the smoke. "The wife doesn't let me smoke in the house." He managed a forced half smile. The bags under his eyes told me he was not sleeping. His five o'clock shadow was more of a ten o'clock shadow. The usually well-dressed alderman wore nothing but his boxers. I was ready for a fight but his fight was all gone. Drained by whatever was taking his sleep.

"Alderman, I left Roy in the woods by the storm water drain. There's definitely sewage mixing in with the rainwater. There's no doubt about it. The more it rains, the more contaminated water is spreading throughout the woods," I said. "The water is infecting frogs and other wildlife. The raccoons are eating the wild life and they're getting sick. It's a matter of time before we get sick."

Alderman Sabatini put the cigar back in his mouth, put both hands behind his head and leaned way back in his lawn chair blowing smoke up at the top of the garage. "What do you want me to do about it?"

"What do you mean what do I want you to do about it?" My hands instinctively closed into a fist. I breathed deeply to stop my racing heart. "You're our alderman. The drain is a couple hundred yards behind your house. I want you to get out of that chair, get dressed and walk back with me to the drain so you can see what's happening to our neighborhood."

He took another puff and closed his eyes. "And then what do I do?"

This wasn't the alderman I knew. Right or wrong, he always has an answer for everything. I couldn't think of anything else to say. He struggled out of the chair, stumbling down the sidewalk, clutching the Scotch bottle.

"Alderman," I yelled after him.

He kept walking. I ran up the stairs and pounded on his front door. Mrs. Sabatini opened the door. "Alice, Angelo's drunk. He's walking down the street in his underwear."

She ran past me and caught up to the Alderman. She grabbed him by the arm and dragged him back into the house, whispering softly to him. The door slammed close.

# Chapter Twenty

I arrived at Christy's Pancake House to meet Agent Peabody. I was a little early but I didn't mind. A neighborhood breakfast joint, Christy's is known for its pancakes and homemade soups. Inside are salmon colored booths, a long counter with stools and a revolving pastry display case.

Since it opened thirty years ago, its décor remains the same. My friend Margaret has been here almost as long. She is a career waitress. I sat in my favorite booth toward the back and Margaret brought me a pot of coffee. She knows me well.

"That was something about the raccoon guy at the talent show. Is he okay?" Margaret asked.

I didn't tell her about Jim Reeney's most recent encounter. No need to start a panic because of that moron. "He's fine. I checked with the ER nurse. He must have a high tolerance for tranquilizers. It's probably not the first time he shot himself with one," I said. And it probably won't be the last time.

"He sure hasn't done a lot about the raccoon problem. This morning both of my garbage cans were knocked over. My trash was all over the street. They're getting really bold. I saw them out early this morning. Usually they don't bother my cans in the daylight," Margaret said, leaning a hip against the edge of the booth.

"Margaret, be careful, don't bother them. I think the raccoons are sick. The one at the talent show was sick," I said, pouring a cup of coffee. "I'm checking with animal control. They are going to test him."

"You're kidding? What do you think is wrong?"

I wasn't sure how much to tell Margaret yet. She lives on Central Avenue, which is on the east side of the woods directly across from Linden Avenue. Our floodwater winds up on her block. If the contaminated water gets worse, Central Avenue will be hit the hardest.

Margaret scanned the restaurant. One of the regulars at the counter was holding up his coffee cup. "I'll be back," she said, going to refill his coffee. She came back a few minutes later. "What's the alderman doing about the raccoon problem? I thought that's why the council voted to hire the raccoon guy."

"Alderman Sabatini's not doing anything," I said.

Margaret sat down in the booth across from me, leaned in and whispered, "I didn't want to say anything. Alderman Sabatini was in here late last night. I think he was drunk. He kept ordering coffee. He seemed really nervous. He kept staring out at the parking lot like he was waiting for someone. We finally closed, and I told him to leave. He was rude and he's never rude to me. He didn't even leave a tip."

"I don't think he's been himself lately," I said.

"I'd say. You want to order something?" Margaret stood back up.

"Not yet, I'm waiting for someone," I said. Margaret went back behind the counter. I watched for Agent Peabody. I thought it was time to tell him about the mail I found at Gary's house. Mr. Hiro wasn't a drug dealer and I didn't believe he was a killer. There was no reason to keep information from the FBI anymore. Agent Peabody arrived wearing plaid shorts and a salmon colored polo shirt. He looked younger in his street clothes. As he sat down across from me, I noticed his shirt blended into the booth like he was wearing camouflage.

I sipped my coffee. It wasn't my usual Jewel Eight O'Clock Extra Bold but Christy's makes a good cup. "Agent Peabody, I didn't realize it was your day off. I'm sorry to make you work," I said.

"Jan, not a problem. I was over at Top Golf hitting some balls."

"Top Golf. My neighbor Helen's daughter, Sandy, teaches at Top Golf. Maybe she could give you some lessons," I said. "I'll let Helen know. She'll tell Sandy." Agent Peabody wasn't wearing a wedding ring.

"Jan, why did you ask me here?" He changed the conversation.

"I wanted to find out if you have any more information about Gary's murder," I said. I was hoping he would pull out his notepad but no such luck.

"Not that I can tell you." He sipped his steaming coffee, cradling the cup with both hands. By his body language, I could tell he was telling the truth. "You know, Jan, you remind me of my aunt Sarah. She raised me after my parents died. We lived on a dairy farm outside of Fond du Lac, Wisconsin. She had a way of getting answers out of me without asking questions. She was good at reading people, but she was also good at not letting people read her. I think you're the same way."

"She sounds nice. I'd like to meet her someday," I said.

"I spoke to the Deputy Director about you after I ran a background check. There's nothing in any of our files about Janice Kustodia. That's unusual. I can usually find something about everyone in our database. When I asked the director, he told me to let it go."

My chocolate chip pancakes arrived. They were covered with whipped cream. I like to put the syrup on them before they cool. Some restaurants serve warm syrup, Christy's does not. I've brought it up to the manager. It would be pretty simple to put the syrup in the microwave for 30 seconds. Why put cold syrup on a warm pancake? Either way I usually make my own pancakes from scratch. I always say homemade is best made. "There's not much to tell about me. Nothing special," I said, biting into the gooey pancakes. The chocolate was melting just like I liked it.

He nodded as Margaret filled his coffee cup. He added cream and two sugars.

"We need to go to Gary the postman's house." I said.

"We've searched it already."

"There's a piece of paneling behind the washing machine. It covers part of the crawl space. There's bags of undelivered mail hidden back there," I told him.

"How do you know this?"

"I might have seen it when I was in his house last week."

"Why were you in the house last week?"

"Agent Peabody, we can keep going back and forth with this conversation when I was there, why I was there but the important point is you need to take a look at the dead postman's house." I paid for my breakfast and his coffee. "Come with me, I'll show you."

When we arrived at Gary's house, I entered the code for the lockbox key. The key slipped out, and I opened the door. Sherman watched me, not saying anything. I led him down to the basement. The house smelled worse than last time. "Here, give me a hand," I said to him as I grabbed the washing machine and pulled it away from the wall.

I popped off the paneling and shined my flashlight into the hole in the wall. Sherman stuck his head in. "Have you touched anything in this room?" he asked, pulling his head back out.

"I returned one package to its rightful owner," I said.

"Jan, that's evidence," he said, annoyed. "This is an open murder investigation. You're interfering with a federal investigation."

"I brought you down here. I showed you the mail. The package I found was for a friend. Nothing you need to worry about. I delivered it to its rightful owner," I said.

"It's our decision what to worry about." He climbed into the small opening. I handed him my flashlight. He looked around. "It looks like the room was flooded, and it smells like sewage. I'll have to get a team out here to sort through everything." He tried to dial his phone.

"There's no service down here. I'll go upstairs." Sherman ran up the staircase. I could hear him in the backyard talking.

I noticed the bag closest to the opening was dry, sitting on top of a ledge. It must not have been sitting down here as long as the others. If the letters were dry inside, they still could be delivered. I reached in and grabbed it. It wasn't wet. I dumped it on the floor. It was filled with envelopes. I thought to myself, "Gary, you little sneak thief." So many undelivered letters. I recognized a lot of the names. Some were open, some were not. Most of the junk mail was left just like Gary must have got it when he was supposed to deliver it. Whatever team of experts Sherman was calling over wouldn't know these people like I know them. They wouldn't care about the letters that were never delivered like I cared. The letters could be tied up for months in some bureaucrat's office. Every letter tells a story. Here was a postcard to the Andersons from their son when he traveled to New York. Here was one for Bob from his brother in New Mexico. It was open. I read the letter. He was concerned about Bob's health and wanted Bob to live with him. He thought the dry air would be good for his lungs. At the end Gary must not have cared about getting caught. He always made sure I had Bob's mail.

At the bottom of the pile, I found a large manila envelope addressed to Alderman Sabatini. The return address was from the Army Corps of Engineers. Stuffed inside it were stacks of crisp hundred dollar bills. I dumped the money onto the pile of envelopes. I slipped the manila envelope into my pocket. Whatever happened between the Alderman and Gary I needed to find out before the authorities did. I'd almost got one innocent neighbor in trouble with them already. Even though I don't like Sabatini how could I turn him in without knowing the truth? I heard Agent Peabody come back down the stairs. "Thanks, Jan, for showing me. . ." He stopped talking when he saw the pile of money on the floor. "Where'd this come from?"

"It was in one of the bags from the crawl space," I said.

"I told you not to touch anything. Don't touch anything else. Our team is on its way. We'll handle it from here," he said.

I handed him Helen's daughter Sandy's cell phone number. I had scribbled it down earlier and placed it in my pocket. "Call her. She's a really nice girl."

He gave me a look, pocketing the piece of paper.

I left through the back door and went around to the front of Gary's house. I stopped at Bob Wilson's house. It takes Bob a while to answer the door. He's told me to just knock and walk in so I did. Bob was sitting in his green living room chair, wearing his bathrobe and his oxygen cannula. His oxygen tank sat next to him. He looked up from the book he was reading, surprised to see me. "Oh, hi, Jan, is the mail here already?" He put the book down.

I sat down on the couch. "Bob, in a way the mail is here. We were cleaning out Gary's house and I found this letter for you. Somehow it got misplaced." I handed him the envelope with the letter inside.

He pulled out the letter and skimmed it. "It's from my brother. We haven't spoken in a while. He lives in New Mexico. He wants me to come live with him and his wife. The date here says almost three months ago. What must he think of me?" I could see Bob was getting upset. It wasn't good for his condition.

"Bob, explain to him that the letter got lost and you just received it." I patted his hand. "Do you want to move in with him?"

"I don't have a lot of time left, and I'd like to make amends with my family. I'd like to see him and his grandkids, and I don't relish another Illinois winter."

"If you decide to move, I'll help you pack. Valerie and Bill will help. Whatever we can do to make it easier for you, we'll pitch in."

I could see Bob's smile through the clear oxygen tube that hung in front of his mouth. Bob worked for a brake pad manufacturer in Cicero for thirty years. Never smoked a day in his life but the asbestos caught up to him. I thought about how our past always catches up with us.

## Chapter Twenty-One

I wrapped the plaid stadium blanket around me. It was cold in the Bensenville ice arena. I never missed any of Danny's games, baseball, basketball, soccer but especially hockey. I don't really care for any of the sports but it was so cute to see the little eight-year-olds skating around on the ice, pushing the puck around. And, the parents in the stands were more fun to watch. They scream and cheer the kids on and get so worked up. Meg was just as crazy as the other hockey moms. Bill and Valerie were also big supporters of the team. Bill was the manager and Valerie booked the hotel rooms when they traveled for tournaments. Last year they played the Midwest Championship in the Wisconsin Dells. We stayed at the Kalahari Resort. We had an entire floor for the hockey teams. Every family brought a dish for potluck and a favorite cocktail. All the room doors were open so you could walk from room to room, sampling dishes. And, I must say I enjoyed a few cocktails myself.

Danny's team won the tournament. We didn't get back to the hotel until late at night. The boys marched up and down the hotel corridor carrying their trophy singing, *We are the Champions*. I think it was about 11 p.m. Hotel security came and made us quiet down. At the end of the night, we were all gathered in one of the large rooms, talking about the game, having a good time when I happened to look up at the TV over the fireplace. It was tuned to the hotel's closed circuit TV channel. The first picture was the waterpark, empty. The next one was the lobby, still empty. The third one was the nightclub. That's where I saw Danny and his friends in their hockey jerseys, dancing with some attractive 20-year-olds. I clicked off the TV and ran down to the nightclub before the parents could see. I gathered them all up and marched them back to their room. One of the older sisters, Holly, who was supposed to be watching them, was sound asleep on the couch with her boyfriend. I shooed him out and had a talk with her.

Now Holly was sitting on the bleacher with her boyfriend, one row down from me. She gave me a nervous glance and a head nod. I nodded back and handed her a chocolate chip cookie and one for her boyfriend. I made a tin for the boys and lemon squares for the parents. I don't normally make lemon squares but James' recipe is easy and he walked me through it. I made him come to the game. I don't think he is much of a sports fan either. He looked cold even though he wore his London Fog camel hair coat and his cashmere scarf. He is a wonderful dresser. I tried to explain the game to James but it's difficult because I don't know all the rules. "James, Danny's team is wearing the white because they're the home team. He's 34. He's a forward. He is on the offense. His job is to go down ice and make a goal," I said. "The other guys stay back. They're defensemen."

James listened politely. When I turned away, I could see him reading a book on his iPhone. I don't carry a cell phone. Valerie has offered to add me to her plan but I don't feel the need to be connected and available at all times.

"Go, Danny," I screamed when he finally got the puck. He is a very shy boy and looked like he didn't want the puck. He passed it back quickly to one of his teammates. One of the other boys on the other team threw his stick across the ice, slid into Danny and pushed him up against the glass. "Foul," I yelled, jumping up. These kids aren't allowed to check. I saw Bill walking along the glass, pounding on it and yelling at the ref. The boy, who skated into Danny, started punching him. Danny lay on the ice covering his face until the ref pulled the boy out and ejected him from the game. Danny sat on the bench. He was in tears. I walked behind the bench, tapped on the glass and waved to him. He was embarrassed and didn't want to turn around. After the game I waited in the hallway for Danny. He finally came out after all the other boys left the locker room. His head hung low, his stick dragging behind him. I knelt down and gave him a big hug.

"I'm sorry, Gran, Gran." He said.

"Danny, you have nothing to be sorry about. The other boy was wrong. That was a foul, and it was bad sportsmanship. He's been ejected for three games," I told him.

"I know, Gran, Gran, but the other boys saw me cry," Danny said.

"Danny, remember we talked about bullies." I bent down to look him in the eye. "There's a lot of bad people in this world, and I want you to be able to defend yourself. I've got your back."

We walked out of the arena. Bill put his arm around Danny and talked quietly to him. Meg was exchanging words with the parents of the other boy. Someone grabbed her arm and pulled her back. She looked ready to swing at them. I looked at my family and thought about how blessed I am to be a mother, a grandmother, and a great grandmother. I thought about how blessed I am to be in a neighborhood of people I care about and that care about me. No matter what Gary the postman was up to, he didn't deserve to die over it. He was a part of our neighborhood. We take care of our own, and I was going to take care of whoever took care of Gary.

## Chapter Twenty-Two

It was still dark out, the clouds floated over the moon. Michael had delivered the papers to the curb. I walked my route, carrying them up to the doorsteps. I liked how peaceful the street is in the early morning. Except for the birds, they start about 4:30 in the morning. I'm not sure why but it's the same every day. Wakes me up.

I started from my house and headed north down Linden. I delivered Anne's paper first. Sassy was in the front window, staring at me. Next is Pete and Monika's. I skipped the next two houses. They didn't get the newspaper. I finished the rest of this side of the street. As I crossed over to the east side of Linden, a car flew down the street, aiming right at me. I stood stock still like a deer for a moment before jumping out of the way. It was a large dark SUV, the license plate was obscured. It came roaring back toward me. I jumped off the street and into the evergreen bushes on the side of Helen's driveway.

The car stopped in the middle of the street, engine still running. Two men wearing shiny suits got out. The sun was starting to come up. I couldn't make out their faces just the lead pipes they were carrying. The larger of the two men scraped the pipe along the street, making a high-pitched squeal. Sparks flew off the back of the pipe. The other man followed behind, pounding his open hand with the pipe. I couldn't run. I stood still. I watched in seemingly slow motion like that split second before an accident happens. My mind couldn't accept what I was seeing. It didn't make any sense. I deliver these papers every morning. I walk this route every morning. That was my reality.

Neither man spoke. As they came closer to me, I held my hands out in front of my face waiting for the first pipe to come down onto my head. As the little man raised his pipe, I gave him a front kick to his groin. His grapes squished like I was making wine. The large man came down with his pipe, just missing my shoulder. I ducked out of his way and gave him a roundhouse kick to the side of his face. That took him down to the ground. I think they were more surprised than scared to see an old lady who fought back.

They both shook their heads and stood up. They came at me again. They were close enough now that I could see their faces. It didn't matter. Their faces were interchangeable with every other lowlife thug I've encountered. All muscle, no heart, soulless eyes.

The first thing Master Trevino taught me was not to be afraid of scum like this. The second thing was how to defend myself against scum like this. He taught me to use their size against them. Martial arts is all about leverage and speed, not size. These two ruined my morning and put me behind schedule. I didn't like violence unless it was called for, and they were calling for it. Whatever reason they were coming at me now, I didn't want them coming back.

The large man grabbed me from behind, pulling my arms behind my back so his little friend could get a good punch at me. I pounded the back of my head into his nose. I could feel it break and the blood splatter. He released me and then I punched him in the throat. I turned around. The little man was holding a butterfly knife, twirling it open and close to intimidate me. As I grabbed it from him, I could feel his wrist snap. I showed him how to properly handle a butterfly knife and then I kicked him in the side of his knee. I could hear his bone crack and ligaments snap as he fell to the ground, withering in pain. I don't like violence but I'm not opposed to it when necessary.

Mr. Hiro ran out of his backyard, brandishing his rake, swinging it and yelling in Japanese. He was able to hit the small man on the butt with the business end of the rake. I stopped him before he could inflict more damage on the two men who were already lying helpless on the ground. "Miss Kustodia, Miss Kustodia, are you okay? I heard shouting. I looked out and saw everything. Are you okay? Are you okay?"

"Mr. Hiro, thank you, I'm fine." As we spoke, the two men bent over in pain crawled into their car. They took off. We watched the car tail lights fade into the morning.

"What happened? Why'd they attack you?" Mr. Hiro asked, holding my arm and looking me over.

I shook my head. "I don't know." I had my suspicions but nothing I could share.

"Please, come sit down." He took my arm gently and led me to his house. Mrs. Hiro was waiting in the doorway. "Please come in, sit down." He turned to his wife, "Amaya, make tea."

With the excitement over, I realized how sore and tired I was. I sank onto their oversized leather couch. "Your wife's name is Amaya, I didn't know that," I said to him.

"It means night rain."

Amaya came back with a porcelain teacup. She bowed her head and put her arms forward toward me with the cup. She smiled and bowed again. I sipped the warm liquid and gazed around the house. They had lived here for almost two years. I never knew her name before and this was the first time I was in their house. It was a cozy little room. Nothing like I expected. I guess I expected to be sitting on the floor with paper sliding doors like when Gino and I lived in Japan. Instead it was very American with its leather couch, walnut coffee table and flat screen TV. In the corner was a small drafting table. Mr. Hiro excused himself and went into the kitchen to speak with Mrs. Hiro. I walked over to the drafting table. There were blueprints and designs scattered on it. I couldn't make out what they were. Mr. Hiro returned, carrying a plate of cookies. I was surprised to see Oreo cookies. "Those are plans for a bridge," he said, noticing me studying his blueprints. "I'm a structural engineer."

So, that's what he does. I sipped my tea and took one Oreo cookie to be polite. "Mr. Hiro, thank you so much." I glanced around the room but did not see Mrs. Hiro. I set the teacup on the coffee table and stood up. "I have to go finish delivering the papers."

"You should rest," he said, standing in front of the door. "Let me call the police."

"No, really, I'm fine. There's nothing they can do. I can't identify the men. I don't want any more trouble. I want to finish the papers and go home." I opened the door and left.

# Chapter Twenty-Three

Later that afternoon I picked up Danny on the corner at the bus stop. After my street fight, I realized that this world was not safe for old ladies or young people. Danny needed to learn how to protect himself, and I knew just where to take him.

"Hi Gran Gran, where are we going?" Danny asked getting in the car. I usually walk down the corner to pick him up but today I drove.

"I have someone I want you to meet," I said, waiting for him to buckle his seat belt. When he was done, I drove the few miles to Henderson and pulled in front of a large brick building. It resembled many other suburban strip malls. The sign on the outside of the building read White Dragon Kenpo Karate. Danny followed me into the building. On the wall were pictures of Master Trevino with Muhammad Ali, Elvis Presley, Richard Nixon and Bruce Lee. Each picture was more impressive than the one before. Danny didn't recognize any of them. "Where are we, Gran, Gran?" he asked, taking my hand.

"This is Master Trevino's dojo," I told him. "Dojo is a place of honor for learning karate. Master Trevino is a tenth degree master black belt and an old friend."

Danny looked out onto the floor, which was covered with gymnastic mats. Floor-to-ceiling mirrors hung on the long wall. A kick bag hung in the corner. Boys and girls his age were walking out of the changing room wearing their white gis. Some with yellow belts, some with green belts. We stood in front of the small front office and peeked in the big glass window. Master Trevino was speaking on the phone. He waved us in. I could tell Danny was in awe when he saw the collection of fighting knives hanging on the wall behind Master Trevino.

He hung up the phone, rose and stood up to greet me. He was wearing a velour track suit, his salt and pepper hair didn't give away the fact that he was almost my age. He looked quite the opposite of a great warrior. More like somebody's grandpa at a backyard barbecue. "Janice, so good to see you. It's been so long. This must be your great-grandson, Danny," he said, taking both of my hands in his. I had called him earlier to tell him we were coming over. Then he walked over to Danny and put his hand out. Danny shook his hand timidly. Master Trevino said, "Son, grab my hand like you mean it. A handshake tells a lot about a man."

Danny smiled and squeezed as hard as he could.

"That's it. That's the way you do it." Master Trevino gestured to the chairs in front of his desk. "Sit down. Sit down both of you." He took his seat behind the desk again.

"I wanted Danny to watch a lesson to see what you teach," I said.

Master Trevino said, "Danny are you interested in learning karate?"

Danny shrugged. "I don't know."

"Take your shoes off and walk over to the side by the mats. You can watch. We have a beginner class starting. You have to be quiet," Master Trevino said.

Danny and I took our shoes off and sat quietly on the side of the mat, watching the eight-year-olds do running sidekicks. Across from us, the young woman instructor was showing some students the first kata, a series of choreographed fight moves. I looked at Danny. He was smiling ear to ear. Then the young instructor did an exhibition of numchuks and sais, triangular shaped hand blades. Danny was sold.

One of the little girls wearing a yellow belt ran up to Danny. "Hi, I'm Rose, are you joining our class?"

Danny turned bright red. "I think so."

"It's lots of fun. You'll enjoy it. Do you want to try the kick bag?"

Danny glanced up at me for approval. The instructor nodded permission. He ran off with Rose.

I knocked on Master Trevino's door. Growing up, I knew him as Tony from down the block. I was somewhat of a tomboy when I lived on Taylor Street and Tony and I always got ourselves in some kind of trouble either with the older kids or the police. Tony went off and joined the Marines. I got married and moved to the burbs. Tony stood up and hugged me again. "Janice, he's a good little boy. I think he will do fine," he said.

"Yeah, Tony, I want him to toughen up. I think karate will help give him confidence," I said, sinking onto the uncomfortable folding chair.

"What about you, Janice? How have you been?"

"I've been fine. We've had some trouble in Woodland View. I imagine you've heard."

"Yeah, I saw the newspaper article. That's really sad. Such a nice little community. Is that why you brought Danny in?" Master Trevino asked.

"He has trouble with bullies picking on him. There's one kid at school in particular who has been punching him in the back."

Master Trevino stood up. "Jan, let's take a walk." We went back to the training area. All the students came to attention and bowed. "I need a volunteer." He scanned the students who were all lined up facing him. They all raised their hands but he already knew who his volunteer would be. "You, Danny." He motioned him to stand in front of him.

Danny appeared confused. He did a half bow and went over to Master Trevino. "Class, Danny is going to be a new student. Let me ask you. Rose, what's the best fight to be in?"

Rose slapped her thighs with her hands, bowed and said, " Sir, the fight you walk away from."

"That's correct, Rose. We always want to try and avoid a fight. If you can't avoid it, you have to be able to defend yourself," Master Trevino said. "The best way to stop an attacker is to punch him in the nose." Master Trevino turned Danny around and with the palm of his hand did a short jab stopping an inch from Danny's nose.

Danny didn't flinch. "The pressure from your palm will snap this little bone." He wiggled Danny's nose. Danny giggled, and the class laughed. "This will cause a lot of blood. It's not permanent. You don't want to cause permanent damage. We want to stop the fight." His voice grew stern, "This is only and listen to me carefully, and only, when you are threatened. Do you understand?"

The students clapped their hands on their thighs, bowed and said, "Sir, yes, sir."

Master Trevino motioned for the instructor to come over. "Danny, this is Michelle. She teaches this class. She will be your instructor. She will work with you right now while your great-grandmother fills out the paperwork. Right?"

Danny slapped his thighs, bowed and said, "Sir, yes, sir."

Michelle smiled and took Danny over by a group of students who were working the kick bag in teams. I followed Master Trevino back into his office.

He sat back at his desk and pulled some forms out of a drawer. "If you want to sign him up, here are the forms that I need signed for insurance purposes."

"Great, I'll bring them back on Wednesday." I knew I would be the one bringing Danny to class because his mom would be at work. I didn't mind. I also didn't mind paying for the lessons to help Meg out. It's what any great-grandmother would do.

"Have you kept up with your training?" Master Trevino asked me.

"I had a really good workout the other morning," I said. I couldn't help smiling to myself.

The Postman is Late

## Chapter Twenty-Four

I walked into the city council meeting and took my usual seat in the front row as far away from North Linden Jan as I could. She was also in the front row but at the other end of the line of chairs. I recognized many of my neighbors. I went up and down the street earlier, knocking on doors, encouraging them to attend tonight's meeting.

The first half hour was dedicated to discussing Prairie Fest, the city's annual summer festival. It included approval of contracts for carnival rides, bands and food vendors. The talent lineup consisted of the usual suburban festival acts, cover bands, children's dance groups and Disney radio. None of my favorites. I did volunteer at the medical tent. Most years I'd dose out Tylenol, ice packs and Band-Aids. Usually nothing too serious.

North Linden Jan sighed and shifted in her seat. She didn't care about the festival and did little to hide her impatience. She raised her hand and stood up, "What about the streetlights? Linden Avenue is still one of the only streets in Woodland View without streetlights. Look at all the crime on South Linden this year. Maybe streetlights could have prevented it."

I bit my tongue. The mayor pounded his gavel. "Mrs. Culver, please wait until the appropriate time to speak. There's time for public comment at the end of the meeting."

I don't know why he bothered. He should know better by now. She spoke up whenever she wanted. And, what does she mean all the crime on South Linden? Lights wouldn't have saved Gary. And, that was the only crime, and it happened during the day. Maybe I should have filed a police report about my street fight but it would add more fuel to North Jan's fire. Besides there wasn't much I could tell. Streetlights wouldn't have saved me from those two either. They were there for a purpose.

Alderman Sabatini stood up and approached the large bulletin board with its enlarged map of Linden Avenue. "Beginning in August, we start excavation for the flood water retention pond. The Army Corps of Engineers have approved the designs. We've gotten clearance from the DuPage County Forest Preserve."

I jumped up, waving my hand. "Mr. Alderman, Mr. Mayor."

The mayor said, "Mrs. Kustodia, please, let the alderman finish."

I sat back down.

"The plans and the environmental impact study have been filed with the city and the state. The findings are all available for public view. According to the study, there won't be any impact to the local wildlife," he said. "Chicago Premium Construction already started preparations for the project. An underground pipe will connect to the rainwater drains on Linden Avenue and travel three hundred yards into the forest where the floodwater will be deposited into the retention pond. The pond will be thirty feet deep to handle the volume of storm water run off. The dimensions are based on a computation of the past thirty years of annual rain percentages. The current thirty-inch drain is not sufficient to handle that volume of water. ''

North Linden Jan stood up again. "What about mosquitoes? What about the geese? The geese problem is bad enough already. Isn't this going to bring more geese?"

"Mrs. Culver, please," The mayor said with a sigh.

Alderman Sabatini held up his hand and spoke, "It's okay. I can address Mrs. Culver's questions. The city will be responsible for maintenance of the retention pond. As far as the geese are concerned, natural plant vegetation will be installed five feet from the edge of the pond, four to five feet high. It's like a natural fence around the water's edge. This will help keep the birds away from the water." Alderman Sabatini paused. "It will keep animal waste to a minimum and will help stop algae from growing. We'll ask as always that residents keep the curb drains free of leaves and grass clippings and any other waste. We feel that the retention pond is our best solution to the flooding problem."

Now it was my turn to stand up. "What about the contaminated water and the dead frogs?"

There was loud chattering from approximately fifty residents sitting in the folding chairs around me. The meeting was crowded, this was an important topic. "What are you talking about, Jan?" One of them asked.

I turned around to face my audience. I reached into my shopping bag and pulled out a plastic baggie full of dirty, stinking water and held it up for the room to see. Floating on the top was a dead frog. "This is our backyard," I said. "Imagine if a thirty-inch drain can cause this kind of contamination, imagine a lake full of this water."

People murmured and shook their heads.

I walked over and placed the bag in front of Alderman Sabatini, who said, "Mrs. Kustodia brought this to our attention last week. Streets and Sanitation went out to the woods to investigate and found there was a leak from the sewer system. It was seeping into the storm water pipe but it's been fixed. They also cleaned out the drain. As far as the dead frogs, the environmental impact study showed no damage to any wildlife including the frogs. I do have to say, however, there have been no autopsies performed on frogs except at the high school," Alderman Sabatini said with a smirk.

A few audience members laughed.

"I can assure you the problem's been fixed. I think we should leave this project to the experts," he said.

"I'd like to see that impact report," I said.

Reaching into his leather briefcase, Alderman Sabatini pulled out and handed me a two-inch thick softbound stack of papers.

As he continued speaking, I read the first page. Now I've said I'm not a reader, and here's part of the reason why. The first sentence started with, "according to government regulation 750.1-2-102 in accordance with the EPA section 7 of t. . ." The study was leading me down a path of useless information written in government speak. I sat down. North Linden Jan walked over and sat down next to me.

"Jan, why didn't you tell me about the contaminated water and dead frog?" she asked in a loud whisper.

"You now know as much about it as I do," I said. "Obviously the city's not concerned." This meeting isn't going anywhere. I was done. I grabbed my shopping bag and walked out into the hall. It was the kind of frustrating night that made me wish I still smoked. Instead I grabbed a piece of beef jerky from my pocket and gnawed at it.

I walked down the hall, looking at the murals on the wall depicting the city's incorporation, founder's day, and the first Prairie Fest. The last mural depicted the day the post office was built. It was dedicated in 1934 as part of FDR's New Deal program. There were smiling postmen neatly dressed, carrying mailbags and standing in front of the building. They looked eager to get to work unlike Gary. I sat down on the wood bench across from the mural, staring at it, thinking about Gary. I thought about not just how his life was cut short but about all the packages and letters that were never delivered. I thought about all the lives that might have been changed. Love letters. Legal papers. Sweepstakes entries.

I left the building. It was time to head home.

By the time I got back to the house, I could hear my phone ringing upstairs. I ran up the steps and picked it up just in time to hear Donna swearing.

"D, I'm here," I yelled into the phone trying to break through her curse words.

"Jan, I talked to some people. The Benettis and the Sabatinis are partners in Chicago Premium Construction. The Sabatinis supply the cement trucks."

"Hey, thanks, D, I appreciate it."

"That's it, Jan. We're not going to talk about this again, are we?"

"No, D. Thanks." I hung up the phone. I sat down at the kitchen table to think about what she said. After I made a pot of Jewel Eight O'Clock Extra Bold coffee and grabbed a donut, I reached for a quarter to do my scratch-offs. I don't have a lot of vices left but I do enjoy a little gambling now and then. If you call bingo, Bunco and scratch lottery tickets gambling. I finished my last scratch off. I didn't win anything. I felt my luck was running out in a lot of ways.

I put on my fleece robe and sat down in my thinking chair. Next to the chair on the small round end table was our wedding picture. I held it up. Gino, I'm really in it this time. Putting the picture back on the table, I reached into my robe pocket and pulled out my notepad and my fountain pen. Holding the pen always made me feel closer to Gino. It was one of his prized possessions. In 1963, Gino was a resident at Boston Children's Hospital. He was on his maternity rotation when he helped deliver Patrick Bouvier Kennedy five and a half weeks premature. President Kennedy watched as the doctors did everything they could do to save the baby. Gino held the poor little boy as he passed. It was the first and last time he cried as a doctor. President Kennedy was so moved watching Gino fight for his young son's life that they became friends. This was the fountain pen that the president carried in his pocket at the hospital. That was August 9, three months later I was sitting on Gino's lap in this chair as Walter Cronkite told us the news that Kennedy had been shot. Gino carried that pen with him every day until the day he was killed, and now I carry it.

It was getting late. I took my last sip of coffee and double locked my door. I usually don't latch the deadbolt but after talking to Donna I knew the people who sent the two men who attacked me. And I knew this wouldn't be the end of it.

## Chapter Twenty-Five

I needed help. It was time to get Agent Peabody involved. I traveled to the federal offices on Algonquin Road in Rolling Meadows. It wasn't the first time I was in this building. You could drive right past it and not know that it was the local FBI field office. It's not like they advertised on the door. I took the elevator up to the sixteenth floor. The receptionist told me to wait and she would get Agent Peabody.

A short while later, he stepped into the lobby looking surprised to see me. "Mrs. Kustodia, what are you doing here? You wanted to speak with me?"

"Yes, Agent." I looked pointedly at the receptionist. "Is there somewhere quiet we can talk?"

"I was on my way out for lunch. Do you want to join me?" He asked.

I glanced at my old Timex, reliable and still ticking. "Sure, I could eat. What did you have in mind?"

"I was hoping you could recommend someplace. I haven't found good barbecue since I moved up here."

"I've got a place in mind," I said. He followed me onto the elevator and down to the underground parking lot. We got into his standard issue sedan and headed toward Elmwood Park, a small suburb on the near west side. "Sherman, where are you from originally?"

"Charleston," he said.

Interesting, I didn't detect a southern accent. "Why'd you decide to become a FBI agent?"

"After high school, I joined the Army. I was deployed for two years in Afghanistan. Military police. When I came home, I went to school at the College of Charleston to study law enforcement. I was recruited by a FBI agent," he said, watching the road.

"Are you originally from Charleston?"

"I was born there and lived there until my parents died," Agent Peabody said.

"I'm sorry to hear about your parents." I thought thinking about how difficult it must have been to have to leave all your friends and everything you knew behind.

Agent Peabody seemed like a very nice young man. I felt I could talk to him. We arrived at the original Russell's Barbecue on Thatcher Avenue. It hasn't changed since it opened in the 1930s. Food is still served on white paper plates. As we walked up to the ordering counter, I said, "Try the pulled pork sandwich. It's really good."

We got our plates and sat at a picnic table in the back. "So, what'd you want to talk about?" Sherman asked. He dug into his sandwich.

I pulled out the envelope I found at Gary's house. I had wrapped it in a Jewel plastic bag to protect it. I handed it to Sherman. He wiped his hands on his napkin before taking it from me. A drip of barbecue sauce dribbled on his chin. I reached over with a napkin and wiped it off. "What is this?" he asked.

"I found it at Gary's house. It's a letter to Alderman Sabatini."

"Where's the letter? This is just the envelope."

"The letter was missing. That's what got my attention. Out of all the envelopes in Gary's basement this one was opened and there was nothing in it." I paused. "Well, there was something in it. The hundred dollar bills. I didn't take them. I left them on the floor."

Sherman put the envelope down. "You removed evidence from a crime scene?"

I paused, thought about it and said, "It wasn't a crime scene when I was there. The house was listed. Anyone could go in there."

Sherman smiled. "We're tracking down the money. What do you think is the significance of this envelope?"

"This is from the U.S. Army Corps of Engineers." I sipped my iced tea, no sugar. I liked it straight. "Alderman Sabatini is chairman of the Flood Control Commission. He would have received the environmental impact report from the Army Corps of Engineers. Obviously he never received whatever was in this envelope. But at the council meeting yesterday, he said he read the report and the retention pond would not have a negative impact on the environment."

"It'd be easy enough to contact the Corps of Engineers to get a copy of the original report. Why do you think Gary kept the report?

And why do you think Alderman Sabatini is moving forward on the project without it?"

"Alderman Sabatini gave me a copy of the fake report at the city council meeting. Obviously he knew about the real report," I said.

"The money, the open envelope. You think Gary was blackmailing Alderman Sabatini and that's why he was murdered," Agent Peabody said.

I was silent. I didn't know how to answer him. He's not from the neighborhood. His kind eyes made me trust him even though he's an FBI agent. "Sherman, I think there's more going on here than poor Gary's murder. We need to find out what was in the original impact report and then you need to speak with Alderman Sabatini."

We finished our pulled pork sandwiches and we headed back to the FBI field office. "You may want to wash your tie," I said to him, pointing out the barbecue stains on the red silk.

"Thanks, Jan, It was pretty decent barbecue for Yankees," Agent Peabody said, trying to rub the stain out of his tie and slipping into a southern drawl.

"You know, Sherman, I never noticed your southern accent before."

"I try to tone it down. It gives people an impression that I'm easy going, laid back. It comes out now and then when I'm upset."

"You take care, Sherman." He dropped me off in the parking lot in front of my gray Saturn.

"You too, Mrs. Kustodia," he said.

## Chapter Twenty-Six

Danny's school called me after they were unable to reach Meg. The principal's assistant wouldn't give me any details over the phone, which made me even more nervous. The school office was directly to the right of the main entrance across from the gym where they held Cub Scout meetings. I took Danny a couple times. He didn't really like it.

I signed in at the front desk. In the old days, you used to be able to walk right in but all that's changed now. I went into the office, and the receptionist greeted me, "Hi, Mrs. Kustodia, Principal Grant will be right with you."

I sat down on the little wooden bench. I felt like I was back in Catholic school waiting for the principal at St. Agnes. The nuns at our school were allowed, let me change that were encouraged to beat us with wooden rulers when we were bad. I think I still have the indent from a ruler on my backside. Donna and I did deserve every smack we got, especially Donna. She's the one that talked me into smoking in the girl's room and stealing a bottle of the sacrificial wine.

I tapped my foot against the wooden bench. I was worried about what trouble Danny was in. At least I knew they couldn't beat him. Not saying that Meg wouldn't give him a smack on the backside. The office door opened, and Meg flew in, and ran up to the counter. "What's going on? Where's my son?" She asked.

"Meg," I said from behind her.

"Gran, what are you doing here?" She turned and looked at me.

"They couldn't reach you. I couldn't reach you so I came."

"What's going on?"

"They wouldn't tell me over the phone. I'm waiting for the principal."

Meg sat down next to me on the wooden bench, tapping her foot. A habit she inherited from me. She reached into her purse and pulled out a cigarette. She put it in her mouth. I grabbed it. "Meg, we're inside a school."

"That's right, that's right, Gran." Meg paused.

I could see her hand shaking. I took it in mine. "Meg, you're really worked up. Calm down. It's the principal's office. We've all been here before."

"Yeah, but not Danny. He's a good kid. He plays by the rules." Meg paused. "I think I might have overloaded him between hockey and the guitar lessons and now karate."

"Meg, you give him opportunities. That's what a good mother does. Let's wait and see what the principal says. Someone went to get Danny."

A short while later, an aide escorted Danny into the office. Meg jumped up and hugged him. She stepped back, examined him as if to make sure nothing was broken and then hugged him again. "Cut it out, mom," he whispered through his teeth. "We're in school."

Principal Grant came out, shook my hand and then Meg's. She led us all back into her office. She sat down behind the desk and motioned for us to sit down in the three chairs in front of her. "Thank you all for coming in. I wanted to talk to you in person. There was an incident on the playground today. Daniel got into a fight with another boy in his class," the principal said.

"Danny doesn't fight. He's never hit anyone in his life," Meg said.

I became extra quiet. I knew what was coming.

"The kids were playing tag at recess and according to Daniel's version, Joseph tagged Daniel harder than necessary and then Daniel punched Joseph in the nose."

"Is that true?" Meg's head swung around to look at Daniel.

"Not exactly," Danny said in a small voice.

"Tell us your side of the story, Daniel," Principal Grant said.

"We were playing tag and Joseph was it. He came after me, punched me in the back and knocked me down. He started laughing. I got up, walked off the playground. He came after me. He grabbed my shirt, pulled me back and I did what Gran Gran said to do, I punched him in the nose."

"Gran, Gran told you to punch another boy?" Meg's head swiveled around to me. "Gran, did you tell him that?"

"Well, I told him he should defend himself. If this big bully is coming after him, he has to protect himself, doesn't he?" I asked. It seemed logical to me.

Principal Grant interrupted, "Mrs. Kustodia, we have a zero tolerance policy for violence. It doesn't matter who punched who first. Both boys will be serving  detention."

It was Meg's turn to interrupt. "Daniel, is this the first time this Joseph has hit you?"

"No, mom, he does it every recess."

"Is this kid bigger than you?"

"Yeah, mom, he's like a foot taller and wider."

Meg stared at the principal and unleashed her anger. "Is this how you run your school? How could you let this happen?"

"I wasn't aware this was going on," Principal Grant said.

"He needs to stand up for himself because you're not."

"You have to understand. . ."

Meg stood up and pounded her hand on the desk. Principal Grant jumped back in her seat. "You have to understand. I send my kid to your school thinking he is safe. That you watch out for him. Then I hear some bully has been beating on him every day." She turned to Daniel. "Danny, you did the right thing."

I interrupted, "See, I told you it would be okay, Daniel."

Meg turned to me. "Gran, don't get involved in this. You're not off the hook." Then she glared back at the principal. "How do I know this kid is not going to come after Daniel?"

Principal Grant started talking but Danny interjected, "Don't worry, Mom, Mr. Trevino taught me how to punch. After I hit Joseph in the nose, he started crying. He's not going to bother me again."

I smiled at Danny's new confidence and gave him a wink.

"I think we're done," Principal Grant said, standing up and opening her office door. I followed Meg and Danny out of the principal's office and to the parking lot. Meg and Danny were holding hands, talking softly. Once again I was proud of my granddaughter.

I went over to my Saturn. "Gran, don't think we won't talk about this when you get home," Meg called over to me. I smiled at her, gave Danny another wink and got in the car.

I made a quick stop at Wal-Mart for supplies. I promised to help Helen get ready for the block long garage sale. I got a case of water, garage sale signs, price tag stickers and markers. I pulled up in front of Helen's. She was already working in the garage, the door was open. Her daughter, Sandy, was helping her sort through Tupperware bins. Jake the corgi was laying on the floor, chewing a bone. Helen's husband, Bob, died ten years ago. I remembered because it was a few months before Gino. Helen was finally ready to get rid of his tools, beer signs and some of his old clothes. She didn't see me watching her but as she opened a Tupperware bin full of his plaid work shirts she held one up and smelled it. She took a deep breath and squeezed it. I knew how she felt. I missed Gino's smell, good and bad. That musky hardworking male smell. I gave her a moment to let that smell linger and then I walked up to her. She saw me coming out of the corner of her eye and put the shirt back in the box.

"I stopped at Wal-Mart. I've got everything we need." I brought up the bags with the supplies. I set them on the card table that Sandy set up.

"I'm trying to divide everything up. Clothes in one pile, tools in another, miscellaneous," Helen said.

Sandy was trying to remove the rust off her old Schwinn bike. "Sandy, are you going to sell that?"

She turned around. "Hi, Mrs. Kustodia." She looked at the bike again and ran her hand along the powder blue rim. "No, I don't think I'm ready to give it up yet. I still have to lose my freshman fifteen."

"Sandy, didn't you graduate?"

"Yeah, but I kept the freshman fifteen. It's an expression. It's the first fifteen pounds you gain as a freshman in college from stress eating. I haven't lost them yet."

"Don't be ridiculous. You look stunning."

"Thanks, Mrs. Kustodia," Sandy said.

"Are you seeing anyone?" I asked.

Helen looked at me. "Jan," she scolded. "She just graduated."

"No, Mrs. Kustodia, I've been too busy finishing my studies and working."

"You're still at Top Golf, right?"

"That's right. It's just temporary until I find something in my field. Plus I get to use the range for free," Sandy said.

"I told a friend of mine that you gave lessons, Sherman Peabody. Did he happen to call you?"

"Jan, please," Helen said.

Sandy shook her head no.

"Are you going to help me tomorrow? I hate bargaining with people," Helen said. "This craftsmen wrench I'm going to price at $3. It's probably worth a lot more. Someone is going to offer me 25 cents or 15 cents. It's going to drive me crazy. I'm going to want to throw it at them."

"Sure, I'll help you. I'll be walking up and down the block. I'll stop in for a while and hang out," I told her, opening the package of price stickers.

"How many houses are doing the garage sale?"

I stopped to think. With all the recent events, the garage sale slipped my mind unlike previous years. Last year I applied for all the permits for everyone and helped organize it. This year I was preoccupied. "I think just about everybody except Bob and the Hiros. I haven't seen Alderman Sabatini and I don't know if the Hiros know about the garage sale. Excuse me, Helen." I thought about it. After Mr. Hiro came to my rescue, I thought it was time I was more neighborly to both him and his wife.

I walked across the street, a couple houses down to the Hiro's. Mrs. Hiro was on the side of the house raking her sand. I was careful not to step on it this time. I bowed and said, "Hello, Amaya."

She was pleased to hear me pronounce her name. Mr. Hiro walked around the side of the house from the back. "Mrs. Kustodia, good to see you. "

"Mr. Hiro, I mean Koji, are you signed up for the garage sale tomorrow?"

"No, I was not aware."

"If you're interested, there's still time to put you on the permit. It's a block wide event. We just need to add your signature. Do you have any items you want to get rid of?"

Mr. Hiro thought for a second. He walked over to his one-car attached garage and lifted the overhead door. Boxes stacked to the celling, swayed slightly threatening to fall. "My gosh, you do have a lot of stuff in here," I said, stepping back.

"Yes, we haven't unpacked many of our belongings. This house is much smaller than our previous one."

"I'd be glad to help you go through the boxes if you'd like to start making piles and sorting through things," I said. Helping my neighbors with projects like this was one of my favorite ways to spend my days. It made me feel useful.

"Yes, this garage disturbs me. I like everything in order. It must be organized," Mr. Hiro said.

Amaya walked over and said something in Japanese. I assumed Mr. Hiro was explaining what we were talking about. Amaya smiled. She was very happy. She started reaching for boxes. Koji turned to me. "This garage bothers Amaya very much also. As you can see, she, too, likes everything in order."

I spent the afternoon sorting through boxes with Koji and Amaya. There were dishes, pots and pans and knickknacks, some were Japanese, others were from airport gift shops. One box was full of beautiful silk kimonos. I held up a white one that was decorated with a beautiful purple lotus blossom. "That's Amaya's sister's kimono," Mr. Hiro explained. "They both studied at the Kyoto gardens when they were young."

"My husband was stationed there back in the 1970s," I said. "We lived in Japan for a while. We visited the gardens. They are beautiful. I didn't quite understand what an art form the sand raking is until I saw it in person."

"Yes, Amaya takes it very seriously," Mr. Hiro said, taking the box with the kimonos back. "Her sister was a great raking artist. Very renowned. She died when Amaya was very young."

"So sorry to hear that. This is very beautiful." I ran my hands along the silk.

"Purple was her sister's favorite color. That was her sister's kimono," Mr. Hiro said. Amaya bowed and took the kimono out of my hands. "They were twins."

"That's even more awful."

"Yes, Amaya continues the raking in her sister's memory."

I knew Amaya wouldn't want to part with her sister's kimono. We continued sorting through the boxes. In the back of the garage was a bag with golf clubs. "Koji, do you play golf?"

He smiled and pulled the putter out of the bag. He did a practice put. "Not in many years. I'm so busy."

"There's a driving range just ten minutes from here."

He put the putter back in the bag. "I have no time for that pleasure anymore."

## Chapter Twenty-Seven

Saturday morning. All the neighbors were out getting ready for the sale. I directed traffic, making sure the street wasn't too crowded with parked cars. I helped hang balloons on the mailboxes and put signs on the corners. I walked to the end of the block and looked down the end of the street. Everything looked good. We were ready to go.

Garage doors were opening. Folding chairs were being brought out along with coolers full of bottled water and pop. The two nine-year-old girls, Becky and Allie, who live in the raised ranch set up their lemonade stand. I stopped to buy a glass and tried not to make a sourpuss face. I did suggest adding a little more sugar.

This is why I live here. This is why I love this neighborhood. The feeling of belonging to a community, being a part of a family. As I walked across the street, Koji and Amaya opened their garage door. Now organized, the garage was ready for the sale. They brought out a folding table and chairs. Amaya was wearing jeans and a Hello Kitty t-shirt. I've only seen her in her purple kimono before. It seemed strange to see her relax. She was always so polite and proper. I waved. Koji waved back. Amaya nodded.

I made time for a second cup of coffee before the sale began. The only houses on the block with their garage doors closed were Alderman Sabatini's, Bob's and Gary's. Gary and Bob have good reasons. I wasn't sure what the Alderman's reason was. You would think he would want to be a role model for the rest of the block. Ten percent of all sales were going to the community food bank. Next to James' house, Alderman Sabatini's house was probably the most expensive on the block. In fact, probably in Woodland View. Alderman Sabatini's house was built in the late 1990s during the teardown/McMansion explosion. Four bedroom colonials next to all the 1960s split-levels and ranches. It stood out, towering over its neighbors.

I knocked on the door. Alice Sabatini answered, "Oh, Jan, how are you? What's going on?"

"Alice, today is the garage sale. Do you have anything you want to get rid of? I can add it to the stuff at our house." I peeked behind her while I spoke. I saw moving boxes.

"No, not right now. I've been really busy."

She pulled the door closed behind her to obstruct my view. "Is the Alderman home?" I asked.

"No, he's out."

"Can you let him know that I wanted to speak to him? If you change your mind, I'd be glad to help you put stuff out."

"Thanks, Jan. I've got to go." She closed the door in a hurry. I heard her flip the deadbolt behind her.

I walked next door to James' house. His friend, Roger, helped him set up his tables. I think he has the nicest castoffs I guess you'd call them. "James." I waved. "I see you have help."

"Roger has been most helpful. I needed to clean out the basement and garage. I have a couple hundred books that I want to sell." He set up two eight-foot long tables piled high with books. I looked through the piles.

"Mostly mysteries, I see?" I said.

"I'm addicted to them doesn't matter if they're paperback, hardcovers, even some old leather bound."

"Do you want me to help you sort these?"

Roger looked over at me. "We're sorting them by genre and subcategory. In fiction, we have mysteries sorted by cozy, suspense or thriller. There's a separate pile for historical, modern and risqué romance." He turned to James. "We should probably keep those away from the kids."

James nodded in agreement.

"We also have a few science fiction novels. And, then in nonfiction, we have biographies, cookbooks, gardening and true crime."

"Anything I'd like?" I asked.

"I've got some." He ran back into the garage and brought out a milk crate piled high with cookbooks. "I've got French, Italian, fusion, Spanish, Asian, Mediterranean, low carb, paleo."

"Paleo? What's that?"

"It's the caveman cookbook," Roger said. "It's recipes for eating nonprocessed foods that either cavemen would kill or pick up off the ground."

"I'm supposed to enjoy that?" I asked. I browsed through the other tables. I picked up a paperback. I thought it was Shakespeare at first. I saw the name Romeo and Juliet. The cover depicted Juliet on a balcony. When I looked closer, I realized the title was Romeo and Juliet vs. zombies.

"Yes, that's one of my guilty pleasures. I love the reimagining of Shakespeare stories with the occult and supernatural. The author of that book, Mr. Sakai, is a very talented writer. He really captures the essence of the Shakespeare story but with more blood and guts," James said.

"Really, James, this is what you read?"

"I love it. I read to relax." James paused. "I was thinking for Halloween this year I was going to dress like a zombie and throw a party."

"It sounds kind of gruesome but I'm sure people will love it," I said knowing that everyone in my house tuned in to the *Walking Dead* every week. I was not a fan. I've seen enough dead, and they don't walk. Then my attention turned next door. "I just spoke with Mrs. Sabatini. I guess they're not doing the garage sale this year. Have you seen the alderman around lately?"

"No, we're having issues. My basement flooded with the last flood. We got into a shouting match with the Alderman while Roger and I were carrying out some damaged furniture from the basement."

It was almost 9 a.m. and cars were starting to pull down the streets off of Spring Oaks. People jumped out and moved from garage to garage. They browsed through the tables. With the bad floods this year, a lot of neighbors were clearing out their garages to make more room for storage.

## Chapter Twenty-Eight

My 4:30 a.m. wild bird alarm clock went off. I love sleeping with the window open but the whole forest wakes up at the same time every single day. I closed the window and tried to go back to sleep. It was no use. I was still sore from helping all my neighbors with the garage sale. It was a success. We made money for the food bank and people got their houses cleaned out.

I threw on my neighborhood watch windbreaker, made a cup of coffee, walked around to the front of the house and sat on the front porch. It was too early for the Sunday papers but I liked watching the sun rise over the trees. A white American taxi pulled up in front of the Sabatini's house. He honked his horn softly. I thought that was rather rude for 5 a.m. on a Sunday morning. Sabatini's front door burst open. Mrs. Sabatini walked out, carrying a suitcase and rolling another. Mr. Sabatini followed her out. He was in his boxer shorts yelling at her, his hand clutching a bottle.

All I could make out was the word Arizona. She ran down the steps, jumped into the cab that took off leaving the Alderman standing on the doorstep. I knew they were having problems but I didn't know it was this serious. I had heard them arguing more and more over the past year. He sank down on the stairs and put his face in his hands. Then he took a long chug off the bottle. When he stood up, he wobbled almost falling down the stairs. He zigzagged down the sidewalk like he was trying to catch up to the cab.

Over the next week, the only time I saw Alderman Sabatini leave his house was to get the mail. I saw the usual delivery drivers -- pizza, Chinese and even Jimmy John's. I thought about knocking on his door to check on him but it seemed to be a family matter and I didn't want to stick my nose in.

I sat on the front porch, watching. My neighborhood was falling apart. Gary was dead. The raccoons were taking over the block. The flooding and contaminated water was going to get worse. I couldn't stop it. Sabatini was no help at all. He was teetering on the edge, looking down into the void ready to jump. I rocked for hours. I traded my coffee for wine. A black Mercedes 300 pulled up in front of the house. Donna jumped out of the passenger's side. Donna was in Woodland View. This is what scared me the most. Worse than anything happening in my neighborhood. My sister had left Chicago and showed up on my doorstep.

She sat in the rocker next to me. "You got another of those?" she pointed to my glass of wine.

I could see her husband, Sammy, watching me from the car. I reached down to the jug of wine I had next to my rocking chair. I filled my glass and handed it to her. She downed it one gulp. "Jan,

Sammy and I are leaving for Italy today, right now," she said.

"I thought you weren't leaving until later this month," I said.

She motioned with the empty wine glass. I filled it up again and she downed it. I noticed the Mercedes was still running. Sammy bent his head down to get another look from the driver's side motioning for Donna to hurry up. "Jan, you wanted me to ask questions. I asked questions. You know people don't like when you ask questions. It upsets the whole applecart, you know what I mean."

"Are you in trouble?" I asked.

"We're all in trouble. Sammy and I are going to be gone for longer than we originally thought. I don't know. We might not come back. I just don't know."

"D, I can help you. I know people. I have friends."

"It's too late for that. We'll be fine. We've got money socked away. Sammy's got cousins over there. Maybe sometime you can come visit."

I placed my hand on her perfectly manicured hand. My nails were bitten down and had a little bit of dirt under one. It didn't matter. For all our differences, we are still sisters. "D, you take care of yourself. I'll be fine."

"You know you can come with us."

"I can't leave my neighborhood. I'll be fine." We hugged as Sammy honked the horn. And then they were gone.

## Chapter Twenty-Nine

Tonight is James' annual murder mystery dinner, a costume party based on the classic game Clue. Everyone is assigned a character and comes dressed as that character. This year I'm Mrs. White. Last year I was Mrs. Peacock. Maybe James assigned her to me because of my white hair. When I asked, he didn't give me a straight answer. He did say that Roger offered to die my hair but I like to let nature take its course.

I quickly dressed into Mrs. White's housekeeping dress. James sent the costume over for me earlier in the week. I grabbed the feather duster to complete my outfit. Looking out my front window, I saw the dark clouds gathering and grabbed my umbrella. I walked the few houses to James' colonial, which is on the east side of Linden Avenue.

After I knocked on his mahogany door, James opened it wearing Professor Plum's purple bow tie, round glasses and crushed velvet purple smoking jacket. I made it in just before the rain started.

When I walked into the living room, Helen was already there dressed as Mrs. Peacock with a large feather hat and veil and fur wrapped around her neck. Helen's daughter, Sandy was wearing a red satin evening gown, long white gloves and carrying a gold cigarette holder as Miss Scarlett. I had made sure James assigned Miss Scarlett to Sandy.

I couldn't talk Bill into coming as Colonel Mustard so at the last minute James was able to enlist Roger to play him. He appeared as if he was enjoying his character wearing his hunting jacket, a safari hat and waving his pipe around while he talked.

James' house was the perfect setting for a game of Clue. His furniture looked like it was right out of the game. His side tables and wingback chairs he told me were from the early 1900s. He found them at an estate sale in London, the year he and Roger took their European vacation. The inside of the colonial is huge, bigger than it appears from the outside with a formal dining room and sitting room.

James calls the greenhouse off the kitchen the Conservatory when he hosts his Clue parties. There is a library and study. Before the night was over, we'd visit each room looking for clues. For now, we listened to James' collection of 78 albums, sipping champagne and enjoying his canapés. The game could not start until our last guest arrived. I hoped that he would show up. Almost 8 p.m. Dinner would be served soon. At that point I was almost certain we'd be short a Mr. Green. Then the doorbell rang. Since I was dressed like the housekeeper, I answered. Agent Peabody looked quite handsome in his green suit. After our last conversation, I could tell he was lonely. Sherman had been here for a few months but didn't appear to know anyone. He didn't seem the kind of man who made friends easily. I convinced him to come to the party by dropping the deputy director's name again. I curtseyed, "Mr. Green, dinner is served. Please come in." I closed the door behind him.

James led us into the formal dining room, the centerpiece of which is a massive beautifully set table. James told me it was Chippendale. It could have been Wal-Mart as far as I knew. I watched Sherman's face when he first laid eyes on Sandy. Her beautiful auburn hair wrapped around her bare shoulders. Her red dress and red fingernails sparkled in the soft candlelight. She is a beautiful young woman. I nudged Roger out of the way and sat Sherman next to her. James stopped me, "Mrs. White, according to the Clue game, Mr. Green. . ."

I shushed him. "He's sitting there tonight. Let it go, James."

James got it and sat down at the head of the table. He raised his champagne glass. "Welcome, all my friends. Enjoy dinner and then the game is afoot." As he raised his glass, lightning struck outside almost as if on command. The lights flickered. Everyone smiled, believing it was part of his theatrics. Did I mention James volunteers for the Woodland View community theater? All his costumes are borrowed from the local theater troupe. Next week, they're performing *Our Town*. I don't know anything about the play but I don't think it's about Woodland View.

Throughout dinner, Sherman couldn't stop talking to Sandy. They were hitting it off. At one point, he looked over at me, raised his wine glass and nodded.

On the opposite wall from me, the large picture window lit up with lightning. I could smell the electricity in the air. I watched with growing concern as I saw the rain was not letting up. Lightning struck again and thunder shook the house. The lights went out. "James, is this a power outage or is it part of the game?" I leaned over and asked him.

There was a flash of light and then another flash of light, followed by an explosion. "James?" I whispered. "I don't want to ruin the game but was that a gunshot? Or thunder?"

James stood up and tried the light switch. Nothing happened. He carried over some brass candelabras and lit the candles. He whispered to me, "Mrs. White, fill everyone's wine glass."

After I finished serving everyone, I sat back down. The conversation continued around me. Everyone appeared to be having a good time. "James, I'm worried about the rain. Maybe we should stop the game?"

"Certainly not. This is the perfect night for a game of Clue. I couldn't have directed it better myself," he said.

"James, tell me is the murder weapon a gun? Was that a gunshot?"

"Jan, I can't tell you. It will ruin the game." At my stern look, James gave in. He always gives in to me. "Jan, it's Colonel Mustard in the library with a knife. That was thunder."

The thunder struck again. This time I was sure it was thunder. A flash of lightning followed it. James picked up the candelabra and left the room. Then he yelled. When he got the candles, James placed a mannequin dressed as Mr. Boddy on the floor in the library. We all ran to see what he was yelling about. James took his pulse and shook his head to confirm Mr. Boddy was truly dead. He held the candle up to his face giving him an eerie glow and said, "Dear Friends, there's been a murder." He placed a sheet over Mr. Boddy. "We must find out how Mr. Boddy was killed and what room he was dragged from. And most important, who the murderer is." The lightning struck on cue again. Thunder rolled. James was very proud of himself.

I knew we'd find clues in the library. I pushed everyone toward the study. James gave each player a candle. He left clues throughout the house like a blood-stained swatch of Mr. Boddy's suit in the study. Then we walked to the kitchen. For those observant, they would have noticed the missing knife from the butcher block holder. As the game went on, I couldn't concentrate. I kept thinking about the rain. The rest of the guests went into the library. I grabbed my umbrella and stepped onto the front porch to look at the street. It was pitch black but when the lightning flashed I could see a small stream of water pouring down from North Linden onto our street. It was going to be another bad flood. Lightning flashed, illuminating the rain hitting the black pavement. I walked down the sidewalk heading north to see how much water was coming. All the houses were dark. I could see into their picture windows, people turning on flashlights and lighting candles. Lightning flashed again. I could see Alderman Sabatini sitting in his living room chair. He knew what was coming as well as I did. I waved at him, he didn't wave back. He was drunk and still mad at me from the council meeting. Those Sicilians hold grudges.

I walked up his porch, and knocked on the screen door. The front door was open. "Have you called the city? This is going to be bad tonight," I shouted over the pouring rain. He didn't answer me. I was wet and worried and tired of his bad attitude. I didn't care what was going on in his life. He has a responsibility to the neighborhood. I was going to give him a piece of my mind. I opened the door and walked into the living room.

"Listen, Alderman, whatever our differences are, we have to come together for the neighborhood. There's going to be a lot of people hit hard tonight," I said.

Lightning flashed, illuminating his lifeless eyes. Blood dripped down his forehead. His nine-millimeter Beretta still in his hand. I stepped back. I thought he committed suicide and then I saw his feet were chopped off.

## Chapter Thirty

I walked into Katz funeral home, the only funeral home in Woodland View. Cascades of lilies and roses surrounded the mahogany casket. The sweet smell of lilies nauseated me. They always reminded of Gino's funeral, and I could not stand to be around them. It was a closed casket. I found the body, I know why it was closed.

Most of the town came out for Alderman Sabatini's wake. The line of people waiting to pay their respects to Mrs. Sabatini stretched out the door. I think more people respected Mr. Sabatini in death than in life. I shouldn't speak ill of the dead but the truth is the truth. Beside the casket were several pictures of the Alderman from different stages of his life, including his high school graduation, wedding day and his Cub Scout troop from Taylor Street.

Valerie and I waited our turn. Directly behind us I could hear North Linden Avenue Jan talking loudly about all the recent crime on South Linden Avenue. I heard her say something about building a wall or a gate but this wasn't the time to engage her or her nonsense.

I've lived on Linden Avenue for over forty years, and we've only had petty crimes. Cars occasionally broken into, some vandalism but nothing like this. Two murders in two months were unthinkable for our street and for Woodland View. Those kinds of numbers were daily numbers in Chicago but not in Woodland View.

We finally reached the front of the line. Wearing an elegant black suit, Mrs. Sabatini thanked us for coming. Supported by her oldest son, Angelo, Jr., she was not holding up well. I did the sign of the cross and placed my hand on the casket. I whispered a prayer. No matter how I felt about Angelo, he didn't deserve to die like this and to leave a widow. Thankfully, his children were all grown with children of their own.

Mrs. Sabatini started crying. I walked over to her, sat down next to her and handed her a tissue. "My Angelo, my Angelo," she cried. "What kind of animals would do this?"

Angelo Jr. put his hand on her shoulder. "Shhh, mom," he tried to comfort her.

"I begged him to come to Arizona with me." She sobbed into the handkerchief. "I begged him to move. I couldn't live here any longer. We had to get out." She continued crying, her sobs growing louder.

"Mom, settle down. This isn't good for your heart," Angelo, Jr., said, throwing a helpless glance toward his wife.

Francesca, Angelo Jr.'s wife, came over, put her arm around her mother in law. "It's okay, Ma. You come live in Arizona with us. We'll take care of you," she said.

I stepped away to allow Mrs. Sabatini a moment. I went into the little kitchenette off the parlor. I brought a tray of cookies like every other well-meaning neighbor. The small room was filled with tins, trays and paper plates piled high with cookies of all kinds. Banquet stacking chairs were scattered around the tables so people could sit and have coffee. Agent Peabody was sitting next to Sandy. She was wearing a little black dress and pearls. She looked adorable. Agent Peabody was taking care of her by handing her a plate of cookies and a coffee. I smiled at him and walked over.

"Sandy, Sherman, it was nice of you both to come."

Sandy said. "Alderman Sabatini has been our alderman for the past twenty years."

"Agent Peabody, it was nice of you to come pay your respects," I said.

Sandy blushed.

"Sandy, do you mind if I borrow Sherman for a minute?"

We stepped over to a quiet corner. "Sherman, Sabatini's feet. That was a message," I told him.

"Jan, not here. We can't talk about this here," Agent Peabody said. I could tell he was nervous, his hands were shoved deep into his pockets.

I pulled him into the hallway to look for a quiet room. I found a door and we went into the embalming room. The guy lying on the slab wouldn't overhear us. "Sabatini was depressed. He was walking around the neighborhood drunk after his wife left him," I told him.

"When did she leave?"

"I saw her take off a couple days ago. I overheard her say she was going to Arizona. That's where her kids live. Sabatini loved her, I know he did. He wanted to go after her, and they couldn't let him leave. That was the message, 'You can't walk away without your feet.' He got one shot off at his attacker," I said. "Did you find any blood other than Sabatini's?"

"Yes, we found blood but couldn't make a DNA match," he said.

"I knew it was a gunshot," I said. Agent Peabody just confirmed my suspicions. "There were sixteen bullets in his clip but the chamber was empty. I could smell the gunpowder."

"How do you know all this?" Agent Peabody said.

"I watch a lot of CSI, can't sleep at night," I told him.

Agent Peabody continued, "I checked with the Army Corps of Engineers. The environmental impact report that was on file with the city is a fake."

"What do you mean?" I asked.

"According to the real study, building a retention pond in the woods would cause damage to the ecosystem and wildlife as well as increased flooding on the east side of Woodland View," Sherman stopped. "There's a ten percent grade from the forest preserve down to Central Avenue. All those houses on the east side of town would be negatively impacted by the retention pond."

"Was there anything about the contaminated water?"

"What contaminated water?"

I forgot that Sherman didn't know about the frogs and the sewage. I explained it to him.

"There's nothing in the report about contaminated water. I can speak with the Army Corps," he said.

"I think the people you need to speak with are Chicago Premium Construction. They are the ones that put the new sewer pipes in a few years ago on Linden Avenue, and I think the ones who sent the message to Sabatini's family. His family has a long relationship with Chicago Premium Construction. The Benetti family and the Sabatini family have mutual business interests." There was nothing left to hold back anymore. In for a penny, in for a pound. I'd have to trust Agent Peabody if I was going to save my neighborhood. I don't give my trust easily. It has to be won but Sherman won it.

## Chapter Thirty-One

I watched James zest a lemon. He was making his three-layer lemon cake with the cream cheese frosting. I was helping by reading him the directions from the Martha Stewart cookbook. He was very precise and felt it necessary to follow every step exactly. I usually add everything based on sight. We took a break for coffee and scones. Not my favorite but James made them fresh. They were good slathered with butter.

"So, I heard the police don't have any leads on Alderman Sabatini's murder," James said, sipping his French press coffee which was almost as strong as my Jewel Eight O'Clock Extra Bold. "You don't believe that, do you, Jan? You know something, don't you? I think it's time you come clean."

"I'm not sure what you mean, James."

"I've seen you talking to that cute FBI agent, and I know you well enough to know that you want to protect our block. I feel the same way, so much tragedy on our little street. Linden Avenue has become my home, and I want to do whatever I can to help."

"James, last year when the survey engineer came out to draw up the plans for the new retention pond I was speaking to him and found out his last name is Benetti," I said. "He's related to a family from my old neighborhood in Chicago on Taylor Street. They have their hand in everything in Chicago – construction, nightclubs, and restaurants. They do everything the Chicago way – bribes, payoffs, and a lot of people looking the other way. It's an understanding." I paused. "I found out that Alderman Sabatini's family works with the Benettis. They have a concrete company. When I confronted the Alderman after the meeting about it, he told me Chicago Premium Construction, the Benetti's company, submitted the lowest bid. As you know, it's a closed bid process. The bids are supposed to be secret to ensure all the companies give their lowest price for the work. I can't prove it but I think Alderman Sabatini gave Chicago Premium Construction the sealed bids."

"How can you prove that Alderman Sabatini was involved?" James asked, checking the timer on the stove.

"I found out through Agent Peabody that the environmental impact study that Alderman Sabatini filed was a fake. The real study states that the retention pond would be hazardous not just to the wildlife but would cause more flooding in our neighborhood."

"That's horrible. How could he do that to his neighbors? His house backs up to the woods next to mine. They've had flooding. Why would he do that?"

"They were moving out of Woodland View," I told him. "The day of the garage sale I went over to talk to Alice to see if she wanted to sell anything. She was very nervous when she came to the door. I could see moving boxes in the hallway behind her. The next day I overheard her and the Alderman fighting. She took off in a cab. She didn't come back until the funeral."

James stood up, walked to the oven to check the cake and then leaned back against the oven door, facing me.

"Alice said she begged him to go with her. She knew the flooding was going to get worse, and I think she knew that they were in danger. Alderman Sabatini was going to leave town, and the people that killed him couldn't let him do that," I said.

He stared at me. "You can't be serious. Do you think the killer thought he was going into witness protection? That he was going to talk?"

"Where I come from either of those is a death sentence."

James came back to the table, sat down. I sipped my coffee. When the timer went off, he pulled the cake out of the oven. He frosted it, decorated it with fresh lemon slices and lemon drops. He placed it on a glass cake platter. "Remember, I want the platter back," he said. "You sure you don't want me to bring it next door with you?"

"No, I need to speak to Alice alone." I picked up the cake platter. "James, it's a masterpiece."

"Thank you. Glad to be of service." James walked me to the door. I carried the cake plate. I left his house and stepped across the front lawn to the Sabatini's front door. I knocked. There was no answer. I knocked again. After a few minutes, I heard footsteps down the stairs and then the door slowly opened. Alice was a mess. There were no other words to describe her. Her hair was matted and unwashed. She was wearing black except for Alderman Sabatini's blue velour robe. She looked like she needed a shower. Not her usual polished self. My heart went out to her. I bore the same pain after Gino died. She didn't speak.

I held up the cake platter. "I thought you might need something sweet," I said.

She paused, opened the screen door and took the cake platter. "Thanks," she said.

"Can I come in?" I asked.

"I'm not up for company," Alice said, reaching to close the door.

"Wait," I said, holding my hand up to the door. "We should talk."

She waved me in. I stepped into the large foyer and stood under the gleaming crystal chandelier. Alderman Sabatini flew it in from Italy along with the marble tile floor. All to make his bride happy. Now the marble floor was covered with brown moving boxes, all taped up and labeled for shipping. Alice saw me looking at the boxes and said, "I'm moving to Arizona. I'm staying with my son and daughter-in-law until my house is ready."

"Your house?"

"I bought. . . we bought a townhouse outside of Phoenix. Originally we were just going to go over the winter months but I decided I wanted to live there all year," Alice said, still awkwardly holding the cake platter.

I took it back from her. "Let's take this into the kitchen," I said. She led the way into her custom kitchen. It was spotless, stainless steel, cherry cabinets, granite counters. I knew she didn't cook here.

Like most Italian homes, there were always two kitchens; one for show and the other in the basement for cooking. This one was just for show. "Sit down," I said. I searched through the cabinets but they were empty. I couldn't find any tea, cups or plates. Alice had packed the kitchen already. "How did Angelo feel about moving to Arizona?" I asked.

She started crying and buried her hand in her face. I walked over next to her and put my arm around her. "Now, dear."

"The last words Angelo ever heard come out of my mouth were I'm leaving with or without you."

"Alice, don't blame yourself. Angelo knew you loved him. You really must have been upset to want to leave."

Alice stood up and left the room. I didn't know if I should follow her or stay. I sat in my chair. A few minutes later I heard her shuffling steps and she came back into the kitchen holding a manila envelope. She handed it to me and sat back down.

I opened it up and pulled out a sheaf of bound papers. It was an environmental impact report addressed to Alderman Sabatini.

"I told Angelo that he couldn't do this to the neighborhood," she said through her tears. "I'm just as guilty. I wanted the big house. I wanted the nice clothes. I wanted the new car every year. He did this for me. For our family. And then he got in too deep. They wouldn't let him go."

"Who wouldn't let him go?"

"Angelo never talked about his work, and I tried to hide my head in the sand. I knew it wasn't right. You have to go now," Alice said, standing up.

Holding the manila envelope, I followed her to the door. "Good luck," I told her. "You'll be okay." I hugged her and stepped out onto the porch. She closed the door behind me and I heard the distinct click of the deadbolt.

## Chapter Thirty-Two

Sipping my morning coffee, I read through the three hundred-page report. The only paragraph I understood was the one that stated increased flooding, wildlife at risk. According to the report, the construction of a retention pond would increase flooding on the east side of Woodland View. Our peninsula, Linden Avenue, received all the rainwater from the surrounding woods then drained out into the forest and made its way back to Central Avenue almost six blocks away. A retention pond would make matters worse.

I finished my raspberry sweet roll from Kean's Bakery and thought about my next step. Alderman Sabatini was dirty like I knew he was. He was taking bribes from Chicago Premium Construction. Gary must have found out and was blackmailing Sabatini. I knew Sabatini wasn't a killer. At this point, all roads were leading back to Taylor Street and Chicago Premium Construction.

After putting a pork roast in the crockpot and leaving a note for Valerie, I loaded up my 2006 Saturn with supplies. I checked my list: Louisville Slugger, check; thermos full of Jewel Eight O'Clock Extra

Bold, check; Stella D'Oro cookies, check; binoculars, check; flashlight, check; pad of paper and Gino's fountain pen, check. It was nearly 3 p.m. before I headed down the Eisenhower on my way to the headquarters of Chicago Premium Construction on Harlem Avenue.

Located on almost a full block, Chicago Premium Construction's lot was surrounded by a ten-foot high chain link fence. There were several bulldozers, bobcats, dump trucks, and semis with trailers. The only office I could make out was a doublewide trailer with a sticker on the side that read Chicago Premium Construction. After driving around, I parked a safe distance so as not to be seen. I took out my binoculars. The window in the trailer blinds were up. I could see inside. There were two men walking around back and forth in front of the window. I couldn't make out who they were. 7:30 p.m. The sun was going down. Lights went on inside the office trailer. I could see sitting behind the desk a face I recognized. It was Christopher Benetti, the engineer I spoke with. His uncle, Joe, was the head of the family and all the Benetti Companies. And, is godfather to Alderman Sabatini's aunt. Taylor Street is a small neighborhood but its reach is far. I made notes in my pad and opened my thermos. I drank another cup of coffee and ate a couple cookies.

Nine p.m. I saw a white panel van pull up in front of the gate. Two men came out from the guard shack and unlocked it. I didn't see them at first but then the motion lights turned on by the front gate. I took a closer look through my binoculars and recognized them. One was small with a cast on his arm, a black eye and bloody lip. The big man was limping, his face cut up and bruised. They let the white panel van in, relocked the gate and returned to the guard shack hidden behind a bulldozer. I watched the white panel van drive up to the office trailer. Then I watched Koji Hiro exit the van and walk into the office. He shook hands with Chris Benetti.

A tap on my window startled me. I nearly dropped my hot coffee on my lap. I turned my head and saw Agent Peabody looking through my driver window. He did not look happy. He motioned to roll my window down, which I did. "Jan, what are you doing here?" He asked.

"Sherman, get in the car. They're going to see you," I said.

He came around and sat in the passenger seat.

"Sherman, what are you doing here?" I asked Agent Peabody.

"I've been trailing Koji Hiro."

"Why?"

"He was a person of interest from the postman's murder. He was spotted near the crime scene that morning. He lives next door to where the murder was committed. And he has a history."

"What history?"

Agent Peabody was silent.

"Look, Sherman, we're too far into this to stop now," I told him. "I can't help you unless I know all the facts."

"Ten years ago Koji Hiro was working as a consultant on the levee project in New Orleans. There were several unsolved murders in the area at that time. The victims were all bludgeoned to death." Sherman hesitated. "Like Gary the postman. That was the only clue that connected the victims. And then ten years later Koji Hiro shows up in Woodland View, a town that has never had a murder. Now there are two murders within three houses of Koji Hiro's." He turned to me.

"Why would Mr. Hiro want to murder Gary or Alderman Sabatini?" I asked.

"That's what we're trying to find out," he said and then asked me. "What are you doing here?"

I handed him the Army Corps impact study. "Alice Sabatini gave this to me," I said. "Gary was blackmailing Alderman Sabatini, and Sabatini was working for Chicago Premium Construction."

"Chicago Premium Construction was the consulting company that Koji Hiro worked for in New Orleans and now in Woodland View," Agent Peabody said. "There was an investigation after Katrina into the construction of the levees. There was evidence of bid tampering and criminal negligence."

"There is here, too. The sewer system that Chicago Premium Construction built in Woodland View last year is supposed to be separate from the rainwater drainage system. But it's not. There's raw sewage mixing with the rainwater. I brought Alderman Sabatini proof. I showed him the contaminated water coming out of the storm drain in the woods."

"You told this to Sabatini?"

"Yes, that was a day before I was attacked."

"What attack?"

"Those two." I pointed at the two men who opened the gate for

Koji. "They attacked me on Linden Avenue but Koji and I took care of them."

"Koji? If he is working for these men, why would he help you?"

"I think Koji is dirty but he's not a murderer," I said.

"Even if he didn't kill the postman or Sabatini, he's still involved with Chicago Premium Construction. They brought him here for a reason and I need to know what that reason is. As far as I'm concerned he's still under suspicion."

I disagreed with Agent Peabody. I believed that Koji wasn't a murderer but my gut feeling wasn't enough for Agent Peabody. "They're starting construction on the retention pond tomorrow. We can't let that happen," I said.

"I can't get a stay order without giving away our investigation, and we don't have enough evidence to arrest Hiro or Benetti. There are a lot of loose ends to tie up. For now I have to keep watch."

"This is happening in my neighborhood. I'm the neighborhood watch," I said.

We watched Koji leave the office and get into his van.

Sherman reached for the door handle. "Head home, Mrs. Kustodia. We're handling this." Sherman got out of the car and closed the door.

I started the car and headed toward home. I reflected on what he said. I didn't trust the FBI to handle neighborhood business. It was up to me to stop the retention pond and protect Linden Avenue.

It was late by the time I turned onto Linden. The street was dark. I slammed on my brakes to avoid what I thought was a deer crossing the road. I shone my brights and I saw Amaya wearing the white kimono with the purple lotus blossom. She was holding a candle inside a small wooden ship. I threw the car in park and jumped out. "Amaya, are you okay? I didn't see you."

She backed away toward her house and went through the side yard toward the back yard. I was worried she was in shock after nearly being run over. I followed her. I watched as she knelt down by the koi pond. She raised her head to the sky. It was a full moon, a clear night as she sang in Japanese. I watched in silence.

"Jan," I heard a voice from behind me. I jumped out of my skin and turned around. It was Koji. He held his finger up to his lips, motioning for me to be silent. We watched as Amaya placed the boat with the lit candle in the koi pond. She placed it gently into the water. It floated across the pond. "Tonight is the anniversary of Amaya's twin sister's death," Koji whispered. "Her spirit wanders the earth, hungry, tired and scared. When she and Amaya were young, they were raker apprentices at the Kyoto gardens. Amaya admired her sister's skill. She wanted to be as talented an artist as her sister. Amaya made her sister stay late so she could practice. They did not see the man until he stepped onto the sand. He beat them until they were nearly dead. Then he turned to Amaya's sister and assaulted her while Amaya managed to crawl away and hide. She watched as her sister's blood, her spirit, poured onto the sand. Her light was extinguished. Each year on the anniversary of her death, she releases the ceremonial candle. The candle represents her sister's spirit. Once the candle is extinguished, her sister's spirit is released to go to the next world."

"Koji, I'm so sorry. It's such a horrible story."

He walked away from me, knelt down next to Amaya, whispered softly to her and picked her up. Her skin was translucent in the moonlight, her black hair shone. His eyes were transfixed on hers. He looked at her like Gino had looked at me. I stood for a moment, watching the boat until the candle blew out. Koji carried her into the house. I felt a cool chill down my back. The woods cool off at night but this felt different. This wasn't a chill from the woods. It was something much deeper.

## Chapter Thirty-Three

"Beep, Beep, Beep." My alarm clock. I reached over to the nightstand and felt around. Then I remembered I don't have an alarm clock. I jumped out of my bed, stepped into my small living room. Out my front window I could see the yellow of the trucks through the trees in the forest.

I skipped my coffee, got dressed and ran outside. I was going to put a stop to this now. I ran across the street and into the woods where the yellow bulldozers with the Chicago Premium Construction logo had begun digging up the soil. "Wait," I said. "Can you tell me who's in charge?" I asked the young man who was putting up the orange temporary fencing. He pointed to Chris Benetti, who was behind the bulldozers talking to Koji.

I ran over to them. "This has to stop," I said. "You can't do any work here."

"It's Mrs. Kustodia, right?" he asked.

"Yes," I nodded.

"What are you talking about?"

I looked over at Koji, who was silent. "This retention pond. It's going to make the flooding worse. The sewer system your company put in is connected to the storm water drains. Sewage is being dumped out into the woods. It's going to contaminate this pond and this pond is going to flood into east Woodland View. I saw the engineer's report."

"You must have read it wrong. That's not what the report said."

"I read the real report."

Benetti was silent. He then grabbed my arm and pulled me away from listening ears. "Look, I don't know what you think you know but this project is moving forward. It's in motion and you best keep quiet."

"I'm not afraid of you." I pulled my arm out of his grasp.

"I'm not threatening you. I'm just telling you that all the permits are in place and we're moving forward. You have to leave. This is a construction site. It's for your own safety," he said, grabbing my arm again.

Koji came up to us and pulled Benetti's hand off my arm. He twisted it slightly. Benetti winced and walked away. "Jan, you should go now," Koji said.

I sighed, knowing I wasn't going to win here. I headed toward Mayor Puccini's office. He wasn't in so I went to his house, which is on the east side of Center Street. His house was one of the first houses that would be hit by any flooding from the retention pond. He was in his front yard, playing with his son, Tobey. He is the same age as Danny, and they play on the same hockey team. "Mr. Mayor," I said.

He glanced up from his game of catch. He knelt down, kissed Tobey on the forehead and shooed him into the house. "Jan, Benetti already called me. The city signed off on the retention pond. It's the best plan for the flood control."

"Mr. Mayor, did you read the report?"

"Yes, of course, Jan, I voted for it."

"You need to read this." I brought out the report that Mrs. Sabatini gave me. He sat down on his front step. I sat down next to him. He leafed through the pages.

"Where'd you get this?"

"Alice Sabatini. The Alderman submitted a fake report. He was on Chicago Premium Construction's, Benetti's payroll. Gary, the postman, found the report and was blackmailing Sabatini."

He put the report down and ran his hands through his gray/black hair. "Jan, how do you know all this?"

"I found the envelope that the report came in at Gary's house. He stuck it in the wall. It was filled with hundred dollar bills. Alice Sabatini handed me the report. I can't say who killed the alderman and who killed Gary. But I do know that if that retention pond goes in, it's going to fill with contaminated water and your house is going to be the first hit."

The mayor looked behind him. His son was sitting backwards on the couch, staring out the window, listening to us. "I'll call an emergency council meeting. We have to talk to the city attorney and we'll contact the Army Corps of Engineers. I'm calling Chief Krundel right now."

He accomplished it all in a matter of hours. I arrived at city hall for the emergency meeting. I had spent the day, walking up and down the street, asking my neighbors to attend. To stand up for our street. Of course, North Linden Jan was the first to arrive. I sat in the front row as far from her as I could. James came in and sat next to me. Then Helen and Marian, Anne Hillstrom, Pete and Monika. Last to arrive was Agent Peabody, holding Sandy's hand. They sat down on the other side of me. He tilted his head close to mine. "Jan," he whispered. "I verified Koji's whereabouts at the time the postman was killed. Once I found out where he worked, I was able to check the log book for the day and found that he was at a job site in Aurora."

"What about Alderman Sabatini's murder?"

"Koji was in Indianapolis, surveying a prospective job site. We have witnesses and his credit card record for his dinner at St. Elmo's Steakhouse and his overnight stay at the Omni. He checked out the next morning."

"I knew that Koji couldn't kill anyone," I said.

"We picked Koji up a few hours ago for questioning. He's at our Rolling Meadows office right now."

The mayor called the meeting to order. There was much discussion about the false report and the city attorney said he would file an injunction the next day to stop work on the retention pond.

North Linden Jan spoke up anyway. "What about the $10 million? What about the grants? How are we going to solve the flooding?"

"Mrs. Culver, the Army Corp of Engineers will be coming out

next week to review the situation. We also need to tear up the streets to fix the sewers."

A collective moan rose from the crowd. "Not again," North Linden Jan said.

"We need to do this to fix the problem," the mayor said. "It's the only way."

The meeting adjourned. I walked out with Agent Peabody. "There's a task force that's investigating the Benettis. They've been in touch with the New Orleans FBI team. We'll find out who killed Sabatini and the postman."

I stopped him. "His name was Gary." I walked away from Agent Peabody to James' car. He was sitting there, waiting to drive me home. I stuck my head in the window and said, "James, I'm really angry. I need to think. I'm going to walk home."

"Take an umbrella," he said, handing me his silver handled walking stick umbrella.

"James, you are a peach." I took the umbrella and watched him drive off. I began my journey down Woodland View Road. I'm glad I grabbed the umbrella, it looked like rain. It was almost ten o'clock. In all the excitement, I forgot to eat dinner. My stomach growled. I was tired and most of all I was angry. Angry about everything that's happening in my neighborhood but mostly angry at myself. I zipped up my neighborhood watch windbreaker. For the first time since I put it on at Christmas, I got the joke. Maybe I'm not the watch of the neighborhood like I believe. Maybe all the neighbors are laughing at me. A 75-year-old woman taking on city hall, chasing down bad guys.

Had I been foolish this whole time? Was I just a foolish old woman?

As I turned the corner on Spring Oaks onto South Linden, I saw Amaya dressed in the white kimono with the purple lotus blossom standing in the front garden, silently watching.

The poor dear I thought. Her husband being held by the FBI. She was lost without him. I stood silent watching as she disappeared through the evergreens. I followed her, standing in the shadows. She picked up her rake, floating over the sand, orchestrating designs with the delicate rake like a maestro's baton directing a beautiful symphony. My heart broke for her.

I was not alone. I saw a pair of red beady eyes, peeking out through the tall weeds next door. The little sneak thief walked out from the grass onto the Zen garden on his way to poach a delicious koi. Amaya stopped, her back to the raccoon. She stood silent. She held the rake up to the sky. She swept around and hit the raccoon with the rake. I could hear its skull crack; its body went limp as it flew through the air like a furry Frisbee into the darkness of the woods. Amaya grabbed her shoulder, a trail of blood soaked through the white kimono.

I caught my breath and stood still, not wanting to be seen. I slipped behind the shed. Amaya walked over toward the shed stepping silently. As she unlocked the door, the motion detector floodlight lit up the backyard and the shed. I watched as she stepped inside. I peeked through the gaps between the planks and saw her carefully place the rake on a peg on the wall next to the other rakes and brooms, different sizes and different shapes. Each one I thought a paintbrush for her garden. Each one carefully methodically placed in its proper spot. I continued to hold my breath. As she was closing the door, I inched over to another gap, a little to my right. Hanging on the other wall, each one carefully methodically placed in its proper spot was a collection of shoes, different sizes and different shapes. On the last peg hung Alderman Sabatini's feet. I stifled a scream.

Amaya stopped, looked around and reached back in, grabbing her rake before turning toward me. I ran for the woods. Lightning struck. The rain started. At first a downpour and then a torrential rain, crashing down sideways. The wind forced the trees to their sides. The small branches whipping against me. My Keds slid as the forest floor became slippery. I fell to my knees. Just as the rake came down towards my head, I lifted James' umbrella, stopping the impact and breaking the umbrella in two. I reached behind me and grabbed her ankle, pulling her down with a thud onto her back. I pulled myself up and ran deeper into the woods.

I couldn't hear anything but the thunder and the rain and my heart. I reached the opening of the construction site and fell into the orange barrier fence. I tangled up into it. Falling to the ground, I couldn't free my ankle. Lightning struck illuminating Amaya standing over me, rake held high over her head. I reached inside my windbreaker pocket and felt Gino's fountain pen. I grabbed it and plunged it into her foot. She fell and slid down the mud of the hill into the open pit. I crawled over and peered over the edge. She landed on a rock, her neck was broken.

# Chapter Thirty-Four

I woke up in a hospital bed, restrained by wires. There was a beeping sound from the machine to the right of me. The Physician's Assistant walked in, smiling. Her name was Martha, and her scrub shirt read Alexian Brothers. "What's going on?" I asked.

"Your neighbor James found you crawling into his backyard. You were in shock, and you twisted your ankle," she said, taking my wrist to check my pulse. She entered the results in the computer which was on the stand by the door. "The doctor will be in to see you." She stepped out of the room.

"I'm fine. I want to get up." I sat up in the bed.

Agent Peabody walked into my room through the sliding glass doors. "Jan, how about you let the doctor decide that?" He walked over, put a hand on my shoulder. I could tell he wanted to hug me but held himself back. He pulled up a chair and sat next to me. "Koji has agreed to testify against the Benettis. He's kept quiet all these years to protect his wife. Chris Benetti knew that Amaya committed the murders in New Orleans. He said he would keep Amaya's secret as long as Koji kept his. I sent the New Orleans FBI DNA samples of all the shoes in the shed, and they matched the victims in New Orleans."

"What about Gary?"

"We found traces of sand on Gary's shoes that matched Amaya's Zen Garden. According to Koji, all the victims stepped on the sand of her garden, desecrating her sister's memory. After the murder of her sister, Amaya went insane," Agent Peabody said.

"Why keep all the shoes?"

"To Amaya, the Zen garden is her sister; the sand on the bottom of the shoes is part of her sister's spirit. That's why she kept the shoes. Koji told us she killed the postman because he walked on the sand that day on his way to dump the mail in the abandoned house. The night the Alderman was killed, he was drunk and walking around the neighborhood. He walked onto her garden. She chased him down to his house. He got one shot off that hit her shoulder and then she killed him. She took his feet because he was barefoot when he walked on the sand."

The doctor walked in wearing a white lab coat. "Jan, before I go I want you to have this," Agent Peabody said, handing me a white card with the FBI shield logo on it. "It's what we call a get out of jail free card. "

I took the card. I didn't want to tell him I already have a few.

"Deputy Director Claypool has assigned me to the Chicago office permanently," he said. "Anytime you need help call that number. No questions asked, and I'll be there."

"Thank you." I pulled Sherman down, put my arm around him and kissed his cheek. He blushed. He started walking away and came back. He knelt down and whispered in my ear, "Did you really know JFK?"

I smiled.

He smiled back and walked off.

Danny ran into the room, followed by Meg, Valerie and Bill. Neighbors made their way into the room after them, crowding it and me. I glanced around at all the concerned faces. Seeing them made me realize why I loved my neighborhood and why I keep watch. I couldn't wait to get back to Linden Avenue.

Vicki Vass

# ABOUT THE AUTHOR

After years as a reporter, Vicki Vass turned in her reporter's notebook to chronicle the not-quite-true events of her real-life Chicago suburban neighborhood. This gave her the inspiration for the Neighborhood Watch series, and the first book in the series, The Postman is Late.

Vicki Vass has written more than 1,400 articles for the Chicago Tribune, as well as Women's World, The Daily Herald and Home & Away.

She lives outside Chicago with her writer, musician husband Brian, their 20-year-old son Tony, kittens Pixel and Terra, Australian shepherd Bandit and seven koi.

Learn more at vickivass.com or follow her on facebook at facebook.com/vickivassauthor.

**ROCKY GRAZIANO**

Leading Welterweight Contender

Mgd. By Irving Cohen & Jack Healy 621 Avenue N. Bklyn, N. Y.

Esplanade 5 - 0644

JAKE LA MOTTA

The Postman is Late